PRAISE FOR

# *Across the Desert*

★ "Readers will soar along with Jolene into the prospect of better days." —*Booklist*, starred review

★ "Instantly compelling."
—*School Library Journal*, starred review

★ "[A] tense, poignant story about the essential nature of friendship and life's unexpected possibilities." —*Publishers Weekly*, starred review

"Experience has taught Jolene she can only count on herself, and she doesn't think she counts for much. But when she witnesses her friend's accident in the desert via livestream, she finds the strength to rescue them both. *Across the Desert* combines compelling adventure, honesty, danger, and love."
—Kimberly Brubaker Bradley, two-time Newbery Honoree and #1 *New York Times* bestselling author of *The War That Saved My Life* and *Fighting Words*

# ACROSS THE DESERT

# ACROSS THE DESERT

## DUSTI BOWLING

Ⓛ Ⓑ

LITTLE, BROWN AND COMPANY

New York   Boston

Little, Brown and Company
Hachette Book Group
1290 Avenue of the Americas, New York, NY 10104
Visit us at LBYR.com

Originally published in hardcover and ebook by Little, Brown and Company in October 2021
First Trade Paperback Edition: May 2023

Little, Brown and Company is a division of Hachette Book Group, Inc.
The Little, Brown name and logo are trademarks of Hachette Book Group, Inc.

The publisher is not responsible for websites (or their content) that are not owned by the publisher.

Little, Brown and Company books may be purchased in bulk for business, educational, or promotional use. For information, please contact your local bookseller or the Hachette Book Group Special Markets Department at special.markets@hbgusa.com.

The Library of Congress has cataloged the hardcover edition as follows:
Names: Bowling, Dusti, author.
Title: Across the desert / Dusti Bowling.
Description: First edition. | New York : Little, Brown and Company, 2021. | Audience: Ages 8–12. | Summary: While using a public library computer to find help for her mother, who is addicted to pain medicine, twelve-year-old Jolene witnesses a friend's livestreamed crash-landing in the Arizona desert and embarks on a journey to rescue her.
Identifiers: LCCN 2021001031 | ISBN 9780316494748 (hardcover) | ISBN 9780316494755 (ebook) | ISBN 9780316494779 (ebook other)
Subjects: CYAC: Rescues—Fiction. | Survival—Fiction. | Deserts—Fiction. | Friendship—Fiction. | Drug abuse—Fiction. | Aircraft accidents—Fiction. | Arizona—Fiction.
Classification: LCC PZ7.1.B6872 Ac 2021 | DDC [Fic]—dc23
LC record available at https://lccn.loc.gov/2021001031

ISBNs: 978-0-316-49476-2 (pbk.), 978-0-316-49475-5 (ebook)

Printed in the United States of America

LSC-C

Printing 1, 2023

For you,
the child of an addict.
I see you.

# NOW

IT'S SO HOT TODAY IN DOWNTOWN PHOENIX, I COULD probably bake cookies in a car. Mom and I did that once—baked chocolate chip cookies in our car. The cookies weren't browned around the edges like when they're baked in an oven. They had mostly melted into a pale hard crust, but they were crumbly and totally cooked through. That was, of course, when we *had* a car.

Racing down the city sidewalk in the middle of summer, I feel crumbly and totally cooked through. Speeding cars and buses blast air in my face hot enough to bake *me*, or at least melt me into a pale crust. My stomach growls, and I wish I had a cookie with a giant glass of cold milk. I'd even settle for a car-baked cookie.

I stop at a bench shaded by a big sign for discount car insurance and breathe for a second, wiping the sweat from my forehead and shifting my backpack full of books from one aching shoulder to the other. If only I had a computer and internet at home, I wouldn't have to make this blazing-hot walk today.

When I finally reach the library, I burst through the automatic sliding doors and stop in the entry between those book-thief-detector things. I breathe in as much cool, book-scented air as my lungs can hold. The feel of the air-conditioning blowing against my sticky skin is almost worth the whole walk.

"Excuse me," someone behind me says. I hunch my shoulders and quickly move out of the way without looking. I rush to the drinking fountain and chug a ton of water before heading to the bathroom, where I throw my backpack on the counter and splash water over my face.

I soak up the sweat under my tight purple tank top and armpits with a wad of paper towels and pull my messy, damp, dark hair up into a bun without looking at myself in the mirror. I leave the bathroom, tugging my tank top down to cover my stomach, but it's too short. Everything I own is at least two sizes too small, which I'm constantly reminded of by the kids at school and by my eternal wedgie.

I slip the travel books I borrowed last week into the return slot, then go to the holds shelf, where several more are waiting for me. I'm not exactly the fastest reader, but when it comes to travel books, the pictures are really the most important thing. I love imagining I could jump inside them and explore all the far-off places.

The computers are mostly taken up by the homeless people using the library as a hiding place from the heat, but I manage to find an open one and set my stuff down. I log in using my library card number and go straight to BlipStream's website. I click on the only show in my favorites and wait for *The Desert Aviator* to begin. Addie usually starts the show around ten o'clock, but never on the dot. I wish Addie would record her episodes so I could watch them anytime, but if I want to see her show, I have to catch it while it's livestreaming.

Since the screen is dark, I hurry to the reference shelves and pull out this great atlas of Arizona, which has a map of the Alamo Lake area. Addie doesn't know that *I* know where she flies. She's never told me—I guess since we've never met in person. For all she knows, I could be some old guy who smells like cheese and onions pretending to be a twelve-year-old girl. So she never tells me where she flies or lives or goes to school or even what her real name is, but that's okay. We still tell each other lots of important stuff.

Figuring out where Addie flies has been fun. It makes me feel like Marie Tharp, who mapped the ocean floor, or Kira Shingareva, who mapped the *moon*. Alamo Lake isn't exactly the moon, but it's pretty cool to discover something, even if it's something small. Even if I'm not the first person to discover it.

But what I really wish is that I could be like Eva Dickson, the first woman to drive a car across the

Sahara. Eva was also an aviator, like Addie. If I had a plane or a car or even a motorcycle (and if I wasn't twelve and could drive and maybe had some money and food and a GPS and stuff like that), I'd travel to Alamo Lake and explore the whole area where Addie flies.

My life is so filled with *If I had*s that it sometimes feels like I'm drowning in them.

I remove the folded square of paper from my backpack and spread it on the desk. It's taken me a whole month to make this map, and I hope maybe even Kira Shingareva wouldn't think it completely stinks up the place.

My map shows the whole lake area with several mines, two canyons, three ghost towns, a hundred-year-old graveyard, native ruins, a bunch of trails, and all of Addie's takeoff and landing spots—stuff that can't be found on any other maps. When Addie starts her show, I'll be able to follow her, not just on the screen, but on my map.

Addie is definitely one of the youngest explorers I've discovered, and I wish I could be more like her—brave and daring enough to go on an adventure. But real adventures aren't like the movies. Real adventures are kind of scary. Lots of people die while exploring and mapping things. They get all kinds of diseases and broken bones and snakebites. They freeze to death and fall off mountains. And this one guy died from a *pimple*. It's true. Totally true.

I already have a few potentially killer pimples on my forehead, and I don't think I could face venomous snakes. Or even, like, a rabid raccoon. It would probably scare me to death. Then again, I don't think there are raccoons in the desert. A hungry pack rat would be pretty scary, though. It might have some kind of disease. And sharp teeth. Definitely sharp teeth.

I tap my knuckles on the desk, but the screen is still dark, even though it's now 10:04. Staring at the monitor, I open a new window. In the search box, I type something for about the hundredth time: *How to quit oxycodone.*

I already know all this stuff. Give me something new I can use, internet. Please?

When I read the words *Oxycodone can be habit-forming*, I want to punch my fist through the computer screen. Habit-forming? Like it's the same as biting your nails or picking your nose.

Fuming, I try another search: *How to make someone quit oxycodone.*

Again, just a bunch of information I already know—help lines and treatment centers and hospitals. I've called the help lines and treatment centers. They always want to talk to an adult, of course. The other day I even tried making my voice really deep and assuring them I was a fully grown adult. They sounded suspicious, but then they told me a bunch of stuff about wait times and cost and insurance that left me with the car-crash feeling.

I type in something new today: *Get into a drug treatment center when you have no money.* But all the websites and information and phone numbers that pop up make the car-crash feeling worse.

Mom and I were in a car accident a couple of years ago. We'd stopped at a red light, and Mom was asking me what we should do for dinner, McDonald's or Hamburger Helper? The light turned green, and I looked at Mom to tell her we should go to McDonald's. We had a coupon for buy-one-get-one-free

Happy Meals, and Mom always gave me the toy in hers, which meant two toys for me—total score. When I used to be into that sort of thing.

But as Mom started rolling forward into the intersection, I noticed that an old brown truck coming from the other direction seemed to be going really fast. As it got closer, I knew for sure it wasn't going to stop, and this feeling shot right through my body, forcing out all my breath and words, leaving me completely frozen. Mom turned her head to see what I was looking at, but she didn't have time to react.

I'll never forget those few seconds when I knew the truck was going to hit us—that car-crash feeling I got in my stomach and chest and throat and even in my arms and legs. Because ever since the accident, I get that feeling a lot. It's like when you trip or lean back in a chair and know you're going to fall. Or when you sit down at your desk and realize you forgot to study for a big test. Or when you're walking down the hall at school, just staring at your ugly old shoes, not bothering anyone else in the whole world, and you hear "Snaggletooth" or "White Fang."

When it hits me, my brain and body vibrate painfully, like I'm being electrified, which somehow makes me feel like I could faint and explode at the same time. I can't seem to ever get totally rid of it, so I do my best to stuff the car-crash feeling into little boxes, which I store away inside.

But I'm collecting so many boxes at this point that I worry about the day I won't have room for any more. I don't have endless storage like a big fancy house. My storage space is more like one of those hoarder houses on this TV show Mom watches. And like the hoarder houses on TV, my insides keep getting more and more cluttered and uncomfortable and stuffed to bursting. I could probably use one of those clutter experts.

Addie's video finally pops up, and I relax into my seat. Even when the car-crash feeling eases, as it's doing now because I get to watch Addie, I feel beat-up, shaky, and tired. I put on the bulky headphones.

"Hi there!" Addie says as always, holding her

phone toward her face, which is mostly covered by her helmet and mirrored sunglasses. "I'm Addie Earhart, and you're watching *The Desert Aviator.*" She laughs. "All one of you. Hi, Jo!"

I smile and automatically cover my mouth with my hand. Looking around the library to make sure no one is watching me, I let my hand drop and hunch down in my seat.

There are some rough camera movements as Addie fixes the phone to the front of her helmet. "Well, I'm still on the lookout for the ringtail, that sneaky procyonid, so I was thinking we'd spend some time exploring a cliffside, where I think there might be a cave. I'll be on the ground today, so I got my snake boots on." Addie looks down so the camera shows her tall brown boots. "The snakes probably won't be out because it's going to get pretty hot, but I hope my boots come in handy. I've heard a snake's fangs can get stuck in them and break right off. How cool would that be?"

I think that sounds very *not* cool. Way too dangerous.

Addie jumps into her bright red ultralight and

buckles herself in. As she starts it up, I bob my feet on the library's thin, colorful carpet. I see what Addie sees—the desert coming at her faster and faster before she lifts into the air. A bushy mesquite tree stands in the distance, and I always worry Addie will run into it, but she makes it over again, and then she's soaring through the brilliant blue desert sky.

Addie flies over saguaros and palo verde trees; wide, barren sandy washes that will turn into raging rivers during the monsoons; and long, winding rivers of green, towering, full trees like cottonwoods and aspens, which are found in the desert only where the water floods during storms. Addie told me all of this. She knows a lot about the desert. I've lived in the city my whole life, so all I really know about the desert is what I've learned at school and from Addie. Our apartment complex has a few half-dead cactuses around the parking lot, and we've found scorpions inside, but that's about it.

"We'll be flying over some pretty interesting stuff," Addie yells over the loud buzz of the propeller. I point my pencil at a spot on my map where I'm pretty sure Addie begins and ends all her trips—a spot just east of a town called Bouse. I think maybe that's where she lives.

Addie flies over a ghost town she calls "Ghost Town Number One." There are a few ghost towns in the area. Checking my map, I figure she's flying over a ghost town called Signal. Addie once landed near Signal and explored it on the show. Mostly it was just an abandoned mine and scattered mining supplies. But she also ran into a diamondback rattlesnake. I couldn't believe how she stood there talking about the snake while it rattled loudly nearby. She said she was out of striking distance, but I think that should be more like five miles, not five feet.

Addie lands her ultralight in a flat open area, and I draw a small star on my map where I think she is. She hops out of her ultralight and lets out a cry. "Look at that!" she squeals. "A wild pig!" Addie chases the pig, and I want to shout, *Stop! It might maul you to death!* But luckily it's far too fast for her.

"Darn," she pants before explaining how she

knows it was a wild pig and not a javelina. "Those pigs are destructive to the desert and shouldn't be here. People brought them in, and now they run wild all over the place. You don't even need a hunting license to kill one because Game and Fish wants them gone so badly."

I kind of feel sorry for the pigs. It's not their fault for being in the desert. They didn't ask to be brought there. And now they're being punished for it.

Addie jumps back into her ultralight after exploring the cliffside, including one small inlet, but no large cave as she'd hoped. She found a gopher snake, a centipede, a few scorpions, and even some bats hiding in a corner, but no ringtails.

"Oh well." Addie removes the camera from her helmet and sighs into it. "We'll just have to keep looking. Right, Jo?"

"Right," I say, and then I feel stupid, glancing around to make sure no one heard me. Everyone is still focused on their own screens.

"It's awfully hot today." Addie removes her sunglasses and wipes her eyes with the back of her hand. For a brief moment, I get a look at her face, her freckled cheeks, her hazel eyes, the wisps of light brown hair coming out of her helmet. Then she puts her glasses back on and takes a swig from the canteen she always carries, wiping her mouth when she's done. "It's supposed to be even hotter tomorrow, so I don't think I'm going to fly."

Seeing Addie is the only thing I have to look forward to lately. What am I going to do tomorrow? I guess I'll probably come back to the library anyway, maybe work on my map or read one of my new books.

"I'm sorry to disappoint anyone watching." She studies her phone. "Still just you, Jo. It's supposed to be like one-fifteen tomorrow, and I could seriously get heatstroke. Then I could, like, get dizzy and pass out or barf while flying. Can you imagine it? The barf would shoot out." Addie dramatically throws her hand out from her mouth. "And then fly right back in my face." She whips her hand back toward her face. "Giant flying barf mess. No, thank you."

Addie's words make me feel queasy. Gross.

"Back to the sky!" Addie announces, attaching

the camera to her helmet and starting the propeller back up. "How about taking a nice little detour over the mud canyon?"

Addie only needs a short distance to get the ultralight in the air, so the open sandy area near the cliffside is perfect. I follow her route on my map as she flies around the lake once before heading toward the canyon. After flying over the canyon, Addie makes a turn, the huge winding green of the wash coming into view.

Suddenly, the loud buzzing of the propeller goes completely silent, like a switch has been flipped, and all I can hear in my headphones is the wind whooshing. It's never done that before while Addie's flying.

And I know something is very, very wrong.

"Mayday, Mayday!" Addie cries. "Coming in for an emergency landing!" The video shakes from side to side, as though Addie is whipping her head around frantically, searching for a landing spot. And then the world is spinning, the desert below a brown whirl of confusion.

"I'm coming down!" Addie cries. "I'm coming down too fast!"

I grab the monitor in both hands. The camera jerks all over the place, total chaos, and no matter how hard I grip the screen, no matter how close I get to it, I can't tell what's happening

Addie is screaming so hysterically that I can't make out what she's saying or if she's even saying words at all. She seems to be struggling to catch her breath, struggling to get a word out. "Huh," she says, which turns into a shrieking sob. "Huh, juh, huh, juh," again and again until she finally gets out what she's trying to say before hitting the ground.

"Help, Jolene!"

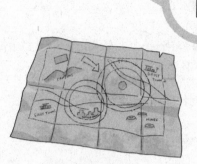

# 30 DAYS AGO

## BLIPSTREAM DIRECT MESSENGER

**JoJo12:** Hi, Addie! My name is Jolene.
I like your show! How old are you?

**Addie Earhart:** Hi, Jolene! I'm 12. Glad you like
my show!

**JoJo12:** Do you ever get scared of crashing?

**Addie Earhart:** Nope! I am a highly skilled
pilot. A true professional.

**JoJo12:** But what if a wing broke off or the
motor fell out or something?

**Addie Earhart:** Hahaha! You're funny.
Professional pilots are prepared for all scenarios.

**JoJo12:** How'd you learn to fly the plane?

**Addie Earhart:** My dad taught me. And it's
actually called an ultralight.

**JoJo12:** Do you live in the desert?

**Addie Earhart:** Yeah. Do you live in the desert?

**JoJo12:** No, I live in the city.

**Addie Earhart:** Hello from the desert!

**JoJo12:** Hello from the city 😊

# NOW

I'm still gripping the monitor, knuckles white, heart
racing, chest heaving. The library spins around me
as badly as the video. I can't make out any more
of Addie's words over the terrible screeching and
grinding and rumbling noises. One very loud crash
blasts my ears, and then it seems for a second that

the phone is flying by itself. Is it still attached to Addie's helmet? I can hear her screaming. It sounds like she's in pain.

Then all I see is blue, the camera pointed at the sky. I can hear her. Somewhere. It's faint. Off in the distance. Over the sound of my own heartbeat and heavy breathing I can hear her screaming and crying and sobbing: "Help, help, help, help." Over and over again.

Why doesn't she pick up her phone? "Pick up your phone!" I cry. "Addie, pick up your phone and call for help!" But I know she can't hear me.

I squeeze my hands over the headphones, pressing them tightly to my ears. I'm getting dizzy, starting to see black spots.

What do I do? What do I do?

My own hyperventilating drowns out Addie's faint cries, but I can't calm my breathing enough to hear her better. Can't think. Can't catch my breath. Can't focus. The video is now an unmoving blue rectangle, but the library spins all around me.

And then I feel a hand on my shoulder, but I

don't acknowledge it. I can't leave Addie. I can't leave her alone.

Now the hand is shaking my shoulder. "What's going on here?" a voice asks. "What's wrong?"

I tear my eyes away from the screen and look up at the librarian through blurred vision, not sure what to say. I point at the screen. "Something horrible," I tell her.

"Oh, no," she says. "We have controls on these computers for a reason." And before I can stop her, she reaches over and hits END on my session.

I whip back to the screen, which now displays the Phoenix Public Library log-in window. "No!" I scream. "I need to get back there!" I frantically type in my library card number with shaking fingers, continually hitting the wrong numbers. It's like the keys won't stay still.

The librarian eventually bends down and turns the computer off at my feet. "Please just calm down, sweetie," she says. "Let's find your parents."

"No, you don't understand," I tell her, frantic to get back to the livestream. I look around, but all the other computers are taken. "Listen to me. There's a

20

girl in the desert. She's in trouble. She crashed her plane. She needs help!"

The librarian looks down at me, her eyes filled with compassion. "I'm sorry you saw something like that. I'm sure it happened a long time ago."

"No, it just happened! Right now! It was live!"

The librarian gives me a tight smile. "I seriously doubt it, and even if it *was* live, I'm sure she has people with her to help her. You don't need to worry about that girl."

"No, she's all alone!"

The librarian looks around at the people glaring at me for making such a racket. "Please calm down. The internet has all kinds of awful stuff." She crosses her arms. "As I said, that's why we have controls—to avoid this sort of thing."

I pound my fist on the table. "We have to help her!"

The librarian stares down at me. "Are you here by yourself?" She glances around again. "Where are your parents?"

I'm wasting time. Addie is hurt. She could be bleeding. Trapped. Stuck. In the hot sun. Alone.

I snatch up the map, then throw my backpack over my shoulder, leaving the new books on the table. I run out through the automatic doors, the librarian calling after me. The hot air hits me like a smoking frying pan, but I push through. There's a fire department around here somewhere, but I can't remember which street.

I run into a coffee shop, panting and sweating. The overwhelming smell of coffee makes my already sick stomach feel worse. The guy at the counter stares at me, wide-eyed. I burst out, "Where's the fire station?"

The guy adjusts his dark man bun and points to the side. "Up the street on Washington."

I sprint back outside without saying thank you or asking for a cup of water, though I'm dying for one. The stabbing pain in my side sharpens with every step until I find the station. I pull on the front door, which doesn't budge, before noticing the doorbell. I ring it over and over again.

After a few seconds, a man wearing a blue uniform swings the door open. "Whoa!" he says. "What's going on? Are you okay?"

"No," I breathe out, sweat pouring into my eyes. "Help. She's crashed. Screaming and I nee—"

"Whoa," the guy says again, interrupting me. "Slow down. Catch your breath." He motions for me to enter a small square office with countertops and computers lining the walls. I'm not sure what I expected—maybe a big open area with firefighters bustling all around and sliding down poles when they heard my pleas for help. Distant voices float to us through an open doorway. I peek down a long hallway, trying to slow my breathing and get my thoughts together.

"Now," the man says, and I turn to him. "You say this is about a crash?"

"Yes." My legs feel weak, and I sit in a nearby chair. "A girl crashed in the desert."

"Where exactly?" he asks, his hand now perched on a phone.

"Out by Alamo Lake."

The man's face clouds with confusion. "Alamo Lake? Where's that? Is that in Phoenix?"

"No, it's over a hundred miles from here," I say.

The man slowly withdraws his hand from the phone. "I'm sorry, but I'm confused. What's happening with this girl, and why are *you* here getting help for her from so far away?"

I take a deep breath. "She crashed her plane near the lake."

"She crashed her...plane? This is an adult we're talking about?"

"No, it's a girl. She's twelve. She flies an ultra-light trike." I hold my arms out. "Like a glider thing. She crashed, and no one knows she's out there."

"Were you with her?"

"No, I saw it happen online."

The man's face clears, like he understands everything perfectly now. "Ah. I see. Do you personally know this girl, or you only saw a video?"

I want to throw my head back and scream in frustration, but I try to remain calm. Getting all emotional didn't help at the library. "I saw a video. But I also know her. I've talked to her."

"And what's your name?"

"Jolene."

"And you live here in Phoenix?"

"Yes."

"So where exactly did it happen?"

"I don't…know." I stand up and whip my backpack around, pulling out my map of the Alamo Lake area. I unfold it and slam it on the desk next to him. "I think she might have been around here." I circle a spot with my finger. "The last I saw, she flew over this area." I run my finger across the large paper, over my drawing of the mud canyon.

The man studies the map. "Did you make this?"

I nod.

"How can you be sure this just happened?" he asks. "The video may have been old."

"It wasn't old. It was livestreamed. I can show you. Go to the website."

The man turns to a computer and types in the address I tell him. Then I log in and click on *The Desert Aviator*. But the screen is dark. "No,"

I whisper. I refresh the page over and over. "No, no, no."

"Where is it?" he asks.

"It's gone," I breathe out.

The man turns to me. "Okay. What's the girl's name?"

"Addie Earhart," I say, fighting back tears, a terrible pain growing in my chest. I know that's not Addie's real name. But I don't know what else to tell him right now.

The man's face hardens. "So you saw a video of a girl flying a plane. Her name is 'Addie Earhart.'" He holds his fingers up in quotations when he says her name. "She crashed somewhere in the middle of the desert, which you saw online, but you can't show me the video because it was livestreamed?"

I bite down hard on my lip to keep it from trembling, but I can't stop the tears from breaking loose. "Yes," I croak, wiping a tear away. "Can you please send someone out there to find her?"

The man shakes his head. "I wouldn't even

know what to tell the fire station in that area. I have no location. No real names. No video..." He looks me over, and I feel the urge to pull my tank top down to cover myself. "Why don't I call your parents and have them come in?"

My stomach drops. I can't speak.

"You said your name is Jolene? What's your last name?"

I stand there, frozen, still unspeaking.

When I don't answer, he asks, "Where are your parents, Jolene?"

I finally find words. "They can't come in." I take a step back. "They're at work."

The man pulls paper and a pencil from a drawer and pushes them in front of me. "Could you write their numbers down, please? I'm sure we can all get this figured out together."

I pause with my hand over the paper. Will they send someone to my house if I write down my real phone number? All I want is to get help for Addie, but I can't have anyone coming to my house. My hand shakes as I write down a fake phone number.

"I'm so thirsty," I say hoarsely, swaying on my feet, grabbing my throat. "Please, may I have a cup of water?"

The man nods as he reads the slip of paper. He sets it down. "I'll get you a cup from the kitchen. And then we'll get this all sorted out."

But the moment he leaves, I'm out the door.

## 3

## 26 DAYS AGO

### BLIPSTREAM DIRECT MESSENGER

**JoJo12:** What else do you like to do besides flying?

**Addie Earhart:** So many things! I read A LOT of graphic novels and eat A LOT of Oreo cookies and build A LOT of airplane models. What do you like?

**JoJo12:** I like reading, too. Mostly travel books. And I like drawing A LOT.

**Addie Earhart:** What do you draw? Fruit bowls? One of my mom's friends draws naked people. I hope you don't do that.

**JoJo12:** 😆 No, I draw maps. It's called cartography. Do you like to draw?

**Addie Earhart:** Not really. My mom says I'm more "left-brained" because I like math and science. She says I could work on the logic part sometimes, though, but I'm not really sure what she means by that.

**JoJo12:** I'm not very good at math. I got a D last year.

**Addie Earhart:** You need to know a lot of math to be a pilot. You know, rate equations and descent profile and all that. What do you want to do when you get older?

**JoJo12:** I don't know. I guess I won't be a math expert.

**Addie Earhart:** That's called a mathematician.

**JoJo12:** See? I told you I'm not good at math. The library timer is about to run out so I better go. See you later, Aviator!

**Addie Earhart:** After a while, JoJo.

**Addie Earhart:** Crocodile 😊

# NOW

I sprint up the cracked, stained concrete steps of my apartment building, dig out my key, and shove it into the door handle. I always have to jiggle the key just right to get the old, rusty lock to turn, and I curse under my breath. It finally opens, and I push through the peeling, warped door. Tossing my backpack on the floor of the living room, I dash into the kitchen, turn on the faucet, and gulp tap water directly from the stream. Phoenix tap water tastes awful, like warm liquid dirt, but I'm so thirty right now I'd drink anything wet.

I run into Mom's dark room and shake her hard, my belly sloshing with water. There's no time to waste being gentle.

Mom groans. "What?"

"I need your help, Mom. Someone needs your help."

She rolls over and faces me. Her eyes are red and puffy, her blond hair frizzy and tangled, the dark roots grown out several inches. Mom used to buy a box of cheap blond dye from Walmart every couple of months—her big "splurge" as she called it. She taught me how to paint her roots with a paintbrush, Mom pretending we were having our hair done at a fancy salon together. Pretending that afterward, we'd get manicures, then go on a shopping spree and eat salads and drink iced tea at an expensive restaurant at a resort overlooking Camelback Mountain, where all the richest families live in their mansions. The perfect girls' day.

"What?" Mom says again.

I grab her clammy hand, tugging on it a little. "No one will help me. I need you to help me help someone."

"What are you talking about, Jolene?"

I take a deep breath, speaking slowly. "A girl is hurt. Out in the desert. She's hurt, and I'm the only one who knows she's out there." I tug on her hand a little more, trying to force her into action by pulling her out of bed. "She could be dying. And it's so hot."

She yanks her hand out of mine and pushes herself up, digging her elbows into the rumpled, unwashed bedsheets. "What are you even talking about?"

"I saw it online . . ."

Before I can say another word, Mom's already rolling her eyes. "Are you kidding me with this? I have enough to deal with."

I flinch at her words and stop myself from telling her she hardly *deals* with me at all anymore. Instead I say, "It was on a show. It's livestreamed, and the video cut off so I can't get back to it. But I know this girl. She's my friend. She was flying her plane, and it crashed. I saw it. She sounded hurt. Really hurt. I don't think she can get to her phone. Like maybe she's stuck or trapped or something."

"A girl was flying a plane?"

"Not a *plane* plane. It's called an ultralight."

"Okay, so call your friend's parents and tell them what happened."

"I don't know who her parents are. We've only talked onli—" I stop when Mom's bloodshot eyes grow huge.

"You met this person *online*?" She slaps her hand down on the bed. "I told you not to talk to

33

strangers online. This 'girl' is probably some creep looking to prey on little girls."

"I can see her on the video, Mom! She's not a creep. She's twelve!"

Mom grabs her phone from the side table. "Show me this girl. I want to see the video right now."

My hair has come loose, and I grip it, squeezing hard until my scalp stings. Why won't she listen to me? Why doesn't she ever listen to me anymore? "I can't show you," I mutter.

"Why not?"

"I told you—they're livestreamed. They don't record."

Mom sets the phone back down. "Where did you see this?"

"On a website called BlipStream."

"No, where were *you*?"

"At the library."

She points a finger at me. "No more library. No more online videos. And no more talking to strangers. Do you hear me?"

I release my hair, letting my arms fall limply at

my sides, and chew my lip. Yeah, I hear her, but I can't possibly agree to that right now.

"Do you hear me?" she says much louder.

I chew my lip so hard that I taste blood. "Yes," I finally whisper.

Mom grabs a small orange bottle from the side table, presses down on the lid angrily, and unscrews it. The lid slips out of her hands and falls on the worn carpet, but she doesn't seem to notice. I can't stand to watch as she pops two pills into her mouth and takes a gulp of water from a grimy glass. "I'd like to beat the heck out of whoever it was that got you worked up so badly," she says, lying back down and curling up against a pillow.

I stand there watching her. She doesn't open her eyes again, and I have to resist the urge to throw the water glass across the room. I trudge back out to the living room and collapse onto our thrift-store couch. What do I do now? Who can I call for help? Who's going to listen to me?

And what if they *do* listen to me? They'll probably want to come to our apartment to talk to us. What if they see Mom sleeping in the middle of the day? What if they see the bare cupboards and dirty furniture? What if they see the pill bottles? Would they arrest her? Would I have to go to foster care? Would I end up there forever this time?

Benjamin enters my mind. I haven't seen or heard from him in a couple of years. He was my friend until they arrested his mom and took him away.

His mom had all those bottles of pills. Just like my mom.

I hope Benjamin's okay, but I don't even know where he is now. I wish he would call, but we lost our old phone number when we moved after the accident and never got a new landline.

So I know what will happen if someone listens to me, *really* listens to me, and comes here. All they'll care about is Mom's pill bottles. And no one will care about actually helping Mom. Or helping Addie.

## 4

I PACE THE DINGY BROWN CARPET OF OUR TINY APART-ment living room. Over and over again, I box up the car-crash feeling and store it away, but it keeps coming and coming. It's like everything around me is screaming. Even the quiet is screaming. And my stacks of boxes are getting higher by the second, like a game of Jenga, about to tumble at any moment with a big startling crash.

Who can I call for help? Who can I trust? Aunt Mallory is long gone, not that I would ever, *ever* trust her again. That was a lesson I only need to learn once. I can't think of a single person who has helped us since the car accident.

I sneak back into Mom's room once she's sleeping again and take her phone. But no matter how many messages I send Addie through BlipStream messenger, nothing comes back. She wouldn't leave me hanging like this if she was okay. Her cries for help echo over and over in my head, and I can still see that blinding blue sky while her phone lay somewhere on the ground nearby. She would let me know if she got to it.

Maybe I can call someone without giving my real name? If I call 911, they'll get all my information. Plus, it will send me to a Phoenix office. I know this because when Mom and I were in the car accident, I was the one who called 911 with Mom's phone while she was knocked out. I thought she was dead. It was the scariest moment of my life—even scarier than when I knew that truck was going to hit us.

Grabbing my backpack, I pull out a pencil and my map of Alamo Lake. I spread it on the glass coffee table, being careful to avoid the chipped corner that's cut my leg a couple of times, and circle the spot where I think Addie crashed. I use Mom's phone to search for police or fire departments in

Bouse until I find a number for the La Paz County Sheriff's Office.

"Sherriff's Office," says the man on the line.

I remember my ordeals with the drug treatment centers and do my best to deepen my voice. "Yes, hi," I say. "I'm a grown-up, and there's been an accident."

"Can I get your name, please?" the man asks.

"Uh…" Again I struggle with what to do. I'm not used to having to make up stuff on the fly. If only Mom were okay, everything would be so much simpler. "Eva Dickson."

"Phone number?"

I don't want to give it because then he can probably look up the owner of the phone, which is Mom. And then I realize he might already have it because of caller ID and all that. But they're far away. They wouldn't send someone to my apartment all the way from out there, would they? I decide to give him the real number so he doesn't get suspicious.

"Where are you located?"

"Alamo Lake."

"What's the nature of the accident?"

"Plane crash."

He seems surprised. "Plane crash? Were you on the plane?"

"No, I witnessed it."

"And where exactly are you?"

I feel unsteady, not sure what to say next. "Out by Alamo Lake. I can tell you the general, uh, vicinity of where the crash happened." *Vicinity* is a really good word. Definitely makes me sound older.

"How old are you?" the man asks, his voice filled with suspicion.

I guess saying *vicinity* didn't make me sound that much older. "I'm...uh...sixty-five."

He's quiet a moment, and I know I shot way too high. Should've told him fifty-two.

"Since Alamo Lake is a state park," he says, "I'll reach out to the ranger out there about this and get back to you."

Just as I'm turning the ringer down to make sure Mom doesn't hear it when he calls back, she emerges from the dark room, puffy faced and groggy. "Where's my phone?"

I hand it over, my fingers so limp I nearly drop it. "Sorry," I mumble. "I was looking something up." What if they call back while Mom has the phone? The pain in my chest grows. Why is everything so complicated? Getting help for someone shouldn't be this hard. Maybe it's only this hard for me.

"Please don't take it again without asking," Mom says, slipping the phone into her robe pocket.

"I won't." I rub my aching chest, wondering if it's possible for the car-crash feeling to stop my heart by squeezing it to death or something.

Mom shuffles around the kitchen, opening and closing cupboards. "Did you eat the last of the Cheerios?"

"Yes, sorry. We need groceries." Maybe I can get Mom to go to the store. But then she'd take her phone with her, and I badly need that phone.

"I'll go tomorrow." Mom yawns and then disappears back into her dark room.

I sit on the couch, trying to get control of my breathing. Sometimes I breathe so hard that I start to see black spots, and I hate when that happens. *It's fine*, I tell myself. *The police are going to call the ranger at Alamo Lake, and they're going to go out where Addie crashed and find her. It won't be too late.*

Once I'm sure Mom is sleeping again, I creep into her room and take her phone and charger. I feel a burst of excitement when I see she has a voice mail. They must've found Addie. Everything is going to be okay. I hurry out to the living room to listen to the message.

"Hello," the caller says, "this is Tim Cedar from the La Paz County Sheriff's Office. We spoke earlier. We've managed to get in touch with the ranger over at Alamo Lake. All planes that have filed flight plans for that area have been accounted for. No crashes have been reported, and the ranger hasn't noticed any unusual activity in the area. If you want to discuss this further, please have a *parent* call us back."

Parent? I want to scream. Why won't anyone listen to me just because I'm a kid? Should I call them back? To say what? I already told them everything. And I'll still be a kid.

I should've known. I should've known it was

pointless to call for help. When has anyone ever helped me before? Never. Grown-ups are useless. I'd hoped that voice mail would take the pain in my chest away. Instead the pain's grown so strong that it's nearly choking me. I hunch over, hugging my middle, trying to focus on what to do next.

No one's going to help me, but I can't give up. Did Jeanne Baret give up when they told her she couldn't travel the world to study plants, even though she was the most qualified person for the job? No. She pretended to be a man and did it anyway. *And* she became the first woman to go all the way around the whole earth.

It's not like I'd have to go all the way around the whole earth. I just need to get to Alamo Lake. This isn't a perilous three-year sailing adventure. It's a quick three-hour drive. No. Big. Deal. And, really, it's for the best that I do this by myself. No adults to mess everything up or start nosing around my apartment. I'll have to take care of it myself. All alone. Like everything else in my life.

The phone battery is low so I plug it in to charge while I get ready to go. I fish the empty gallon milk jug out of the garbage and fill it with tap water, then grab what little snacks I can find—some saltine crackers, a can of sardines, and the stale butt of a loaf of bread. Totally gross. But this should only take a few hours. Maybe I won't even need to eat at all.

I sift through the junk drawer, making too much noise, searching for anything at all I can use, but it's just a bunch of rubber bands and paper clips and mail, *Past Due* stamped on some of it in big red letters. I find Mom's old cracked sunglasses and pull them out, along with a little spiral notebook and a few extra rubber bands for my hair.

I stuff everything into my backpack, along with the neatly folded map, and sit down at our small kitchen table, my pencil hovering over the paper I ripped out of the notebook, my hands still shaking. I rub them together, trying to get them to settle enough to write. Am I really going to do this? I think of all the trouble I might get into. But none of it compares with having to know I left Addie to die. I can't live with that. So I write Mom a letter.

Dear Mom,

I'm sorry for what I'm about to do. I'm going to help my friend. She needs me, and I don't have many friends. Did you even know that?

You always used to tell me that we should do everything we can to help people. That no matter how little we had, there were still ways for us to do good. I tried to ask you for help, but you wouldn't listen. No one will listen. Now I have no choice.

I promise I won't let anything happen to your phone. And I'm really sorry I took your credit card, but I think I'll need it to get to where I'm going. I'll pay you back for any money I use. I shouldn't be gone very long— not even a whole day.

I stop. I can end the letter here, or I can keep going and tell Mom the thing I've been wanting to tell her for a long time. It's easier to say it in writing, right? So I just say it.

I miss you. It's like you've turned into someone else. And that someone else isn't my mom. She doesn't seem to care about anything—not her favorite food like supreme pizza and Dr Pepper, not sketching, not her job, and not someone in need of help. She doesn't even care about me.

I'm sorry.

Jolene

# 23 DAYS AGO

## BLIPSTREAM DIRECT MESSENGER

**JoJo12:** You doing a show today? I'm waiting at the library to watch you.

**Addie Earhart:** Can't. My mom took the day off for a "girls' day."

**JoJo12:** What are you doing?

**Addie Earhart:** Usually we go to the library and go grocery shopping. Sometimes we'll eat fried chicken from the deli in the grocery store's dining area, which is really just a booth between the bread rolls and salads. I wish we had a mall or something. My town is soooooooooo boring. You're lucky you live in Phoenix.

**JoJo12:** Why? I hate it here.

**Addie Earhart:** But there's so much to do! You have an airplane museum. And the air show!

**JoJo12:** I've never done either of those.

**Addie Earhart:** You should make your mom take you. Oh, I gotta go. Time for girls' day out 🙄

**JoJo12:** See you later, Aviator!

**Addie Earhart:** After a while, tacodile.

**Addie Earhart:** I think that's a crocodile that likes tacos, but I'm not totally sure. A tacophile must be a person who likes tacos. Do you like tacos?

**JoJo12:** Yes!

**Addie Earhart:** OK, good. Because otherwise I would've been like FRIENDSHIP OVER. After a while then, tacophile.

# NOW

I am on the city bus. By myself.

I've never ridden the bus by myself before. I can smell every single sweaty person on here, including my own sweaty self. I put Mom's old sunglasses on, doing my best to look older. *Incognito.*

A woman wearing her bra and underpants on the outside of her clothes just got on, and I'm pretty sure the guy across from me has a rabid pack rat in his fanny pack because it's *moving.* Of course lots of regular-looking people are on the bus, but those two are the real standouts.

I study the map on Mom's phone, hoping no one tries to pull something like throwing a rabid pack rat in my face to distract me so they can steal my backpack. I also hope I'm on the right bus, heading for the Greyhound station. I googled *How to get to Alamo Lake from Phoenix* but didn't find anything except a comment on a discussion board about the Greyhound. The Greyhound website was pretty easy to figure out, but the only ticket I could find was to Quartzsite, which is kind of close to Alamo Lake but still out of the way.

I bought the soonest ticket I could find, using Mom's name and credit card. The first credit card I tried wouldn't work, but the second one luckily did. I'm definitely going to pay her back, no matter what I have to do. Sometimes our neighbor will pay me three dollars an hour to watch her baby, and that baby cries *a lot*. So I start a list in my notebook: what I owe Mom.

"Where are you heading all by yourself?" Rabid Pack Rat–Fanny Pack Guy asks me. My stomach tightens up, and I quickly get up and move toward the back away from him, my stomach loosening only a little when the bus screeches to a stop at the Greyhound station.

The phone says it's six o'clock, and my bus doesn't leave until seven. That's okay—it will give me some time to search online about how to get from Quartzsite to Wenden, the nearest town to Alamo Lake. Hurrying into the bus station, I keep my head down, careful not to make eye contact with anyone, and sit down on the far end of a row of blue chairs.

I pull the phone back out and begin my search, but nothing pops up, and my chest starts to hurt again. "No biggie," I whisper to myself. I'll figure it out when I get there. If Quartzsite has a Greyhound station, surely it's big enough to have taxis or Uber or something like that. Mom never takes Uber because she says it's too expensive. I wonder how much money Mom is allowed to spend on her credit card. What if I get there and it won't work anymore?

Someone suddenly flops down in the chair next to mine, even though plenty of other seats are open. I glance to the side and see cutoff jean shorts and pale white legs. I quickly move my eyes back to my phone.

"Hey," the girl mumbles, and I look up. Her head is shaved up past her ears, and the longer blond hair at the top is streaked with blue dye and styled in a sort of hair-sprayed wave.

I look back down at my phone, hoping she'll get up and leave. I really wish people would stop talking to me, especially old people. The girl doesn't look *that* old—she's probably a teenager—but why is she talking to me in the first place?

"Can I borrow your phone?" she asks.

That's it. I knew it. She wants to steal my phone. No way can I let that happen. I stare at my lap, slowly lean over, and slip the phone into the front pocket of my backpack.

"Can you hear me?" the girl asks. "Hello? I need to call someone. My phone's not working."

It sounds like she's telling the truth, but I'm still not sure if I should trust her. "Really?" I ask.

The girl runs a hand through her blue-streaked hair and sighs. "Yep, I dropped it in the toilet." She rolls her eyes. *"Again."*

There's really dangerous bacteria in toilets. Plus, it's super gross. I stare at her hands. "Did you take it out?" I ask.

"Well, yeah!" She holds her hands up. "It all happened so fast. What was I supposed to do? It slipped right out of my hands, went directly between my legs like mail through a slot, and I was like…" She squints at me, like she's trying to figure something out. "I was like 'Cuss!' and grabbed it, but it was too late. Already all full of disgusting toilet water." She rubs her hands over her loose black tank top like she's still trying to clean them off.

"You said *cuss?*"

"No, I said a cuss word—a good one, too—but

I'm not going to repeat it to a little kid because I'm a responsible human being. Except for the whole dropping my phone in the toilet thing."

I sit up straighter. "I'm not a little kid."

"You look pretty little."

I press my lips together. "So did you drop it in the toilet before or after you...you know?"

She shrugs. "It was more like during."

I wince. "Number one or number two?"

The girl laughs, and it totally changes her face. Her dark brown eyes crinkle up, and she has really nice straight white teeth. I bet she's had braces. *Lucky.*

"Number one," she says.

"Can I see it?"

Her mouth drops open. "You want to see my pee?"

I giggle and then quickly cover my mouth so she can't see my own smile. "No, your phone."

She sighs and pulls a wadded up bundle out of her bag. She unrolls the paper towels to reveal a phone, which she grips at one corner between the paper. A drop of water falls from it. "See? I guess that's what I get for texting while I pee. Oh, and that's toilet water dripping on your shoe." She shrugs. "Sorry, but you demanded the evidence."

I resist the urge to run to the bathroom and scrub my ragged sneaker with soap and hot water. Moving my feet to avoid more toilet water drips, I reach into my backpack and pull out the phone. Handing it over reluctantly, I tell her, "I'll scream if you try to steal it."

The girl laughs again, taking the phone from me. "You're funny. What's your name?"

"Jolene."

She sticks out her hand, chipped blue polish on her nails. "I'm Marty."

I stare at her hand, not sure what to do. Toilet. Water. Hands.

Marty rolls her eyes and once again wipes her hand on her black tank top before sticking it back out. "I swear I washed them."

I shake her hand. Then Marty dials the phone and holds it up to her ear, which has about six piercings in it and a hoop around the top. "Yeah, I just wanted to let you know I'm at the station," she says.

"I should get there around ten." She says a couple of "uh-huh"s and ends the conversation with "I love you, too" before handing the phone back to me.

"Was that your boyfriend or something?" I ask, putting the phone in my backpack. Teenagers are always obsessed with their boyfriends.

"Hardly." She smiles. "It was my dad. He likes me to check in with him, and now I won't be able to call him until I get to my grandpa's. I go about once a month—to my grandpa's. He's pretty old and needs help with cleaning and cooking and grocery shopping and all that." She looks me up and down. "So what are you doing here anyway?"

"Going on a bus."

"Well, duh," says Marty. Then she gazes around the bus station. "Are you here alone?"

How do I answer this question? And should I answer it? "Why?"

Marty smirks. "I'll take that as a yes."

"So?"

"So? How do you plan on getting on the bus?"

"What do you mean?"

"You're too young to travel alone."

"No, I'm not. I have a ticket."

"Well, where is it?"

I pull my phone back out and find the ticket in my email. I hold it up to show her.

She grabs the phone and scrolls down the page, tapping her black boots on the gray linoleum floor. "Oh, you're going to Quartzsite like me." I reach for the phone, but Marty moves it away. "Didn't you say your name is Jolene? That's not the name on this ticket. *And* it doesn't say you're an unaccompanied minor."

"So?" I finally manage to snatch the phone away from her.

"So, they might stop you when you try to get on the bus."

"What?" That's the *worst* thing that could happen. "Why would they do that?"

"Like I said. Because you're an unaccompanied minor, even if your ticket doesn't say so." She raises an eyebrow. "It's pretty obvious."

"How old are *you*?"

"Seventeen."

"Are you a minor…company…thingy?"

Marty smiles, flashing her perfect white teeth. "Nope. You only need to be seventeen to travel alone. Anyway, they never ID me—probably because I'm here all the time." She sticks her chin out. "Plus, I look *way* older. Don't you think?"

I shrug. "I dunno. I kind of think you look seventeen." I swing my grimy shoes back and forth and kick the chair legs. My plan's already getting all messed up. "Shoot," I whisper.

"Look," says Marty. "You can get on with me so you don't look so...unaccompanied. Then we can sit together, too. That way some old creeper doesn't try to sit with us."

"Yeah, okay."

"So why are you going to Quartzsite?"

I swallow. "I'm going to help someone, too."

"How old are you anyway? Like ten?"

I am offended to my very core. I look way older than that, even if my clothes are from when I *was* ten. "I'm twelve."

"That's *barely* older than ten."

"It's way older than ten. It's not like you're forty or something. Oh, can you drive?"

"I have my permit, but not my license."

*Dang.* I'd hoped I could maybe get Marty to drive me to Alamo Lake somehow once we got to Quartzsite. "How come you're seventeen and don't have your license yet?"

"Stop interrogating me, lady," Marty snaps.

I hunch down in my seat. "Sorry," I mumble.

Marty laughs. "I'm joking with you. I just haven't gotten around to it. I walk a lot in the city and can take the bus. Why?"

"I might need a ride when we get to Quartzsite."

She scowls. "You don't have a ride set up?"

"Oh, yes, I do," I say quickly, squeezing my hands together. "But, you know, it's going to be late, and I don't know...Maybe they'll forget. Or fall asleep. They're really deep sleepers." I don't know if I'll ever get good at this lying thing.

Marty's mouth drops open. "I certainly hope they don't forget the *small child* they're supposed to pick up at the bus stop. And I'd love to help, but I can't drive without an adult. I know how to drive my grandpa's car, but he has to be with me, and he'll probably be asleep when we get there. He doesn't have a lot of energy these days, except when Josefina's sitting on her front porch. He always goes outside to do yard work when she's out there. I've seen him move this one rock around about a hundred times. I think he's showing off his muscles."

I have no idea what she's talking about, and I don't care. All I care about is getting to Addie. This would all be so much easier if I were older. If I had a car. If I had money. If I had a mom at home who was like she was before the car accident. If people would actually listen to me. I let out a big sigh. "I can't wait until I'm an adult and can do what I want," I mutter.

"Only one more year for me." Marty stares dramatically off into the distance. "Sweet freedom."

"I still have six more years."

"What are you, like, in middle school?"

"Starting this coming year."

Marty grimaces. "Sorry. Middle school is the worst. Prepare yourself."

Her words make me feel sick. How could middle school possibly be worse than elementary school? "So high school is better than middle school?"

She shrugs. "It all sucks. I can't wait to go to college."

"I wish I could go to college."

"Why couldn't you?"

"No money."

"There's financial aid," says Marty. "Plus, I'm getting scholarships to cover the rest."

"How?"

"By kicking—" Marty stops herself. "Cuss."

"YOUR NAME IS KIND OF FUNNY," I TELL MARTY ONCE WE find our seats on the bus.

She gapes at me, and I suspect I've said something seriously wrong. "Why?"

"U-uh," I stutter. "It sounds like a boy's name."

"And what's wrong with that?"

I crouch down in my seat. This Marty is kind of scary. "Nothing. Nothing at all."

"And what about your name?" she says, pulling a pack of gum out her bag and offering me a stick.

I take it, hoping the minty flavor might ease my building nausea. "What about my name?"

"It's a Dolly Parton song."

I pop the gum in my mouth and chew. "Who's Dolly Parton?"

Marty shakes her head, returning the gum to her bag before shoving it under the seat in front of her. "Kids these days," she mumbles.

I look around at the few faces I can see—an old woman with her head already hung forward in sleep, a young Black guy who hasn't done anything but stare at his phone since we got on the bus, a skinny white guy who constantly fidgets and looks around—and a few other people hidden in their seats. I can only see the tops of most of their heads, and someone's wearing a really big cowboy hat that's as wide as two whole seats.

Suddenly, a guy covered in tinfoil walks down the aisle past us. His arms, legs, and middle are totally wrapped in the stuff, and a tinfoil hat sits atop his head. He steps into the bathroom at the back and cracks the door, his wide eyes peering out.

I turn to Marty, but she doesn't seem concerned. "That's just Steve," she says. "He's always on here fleeing the CIA." I must look confused.

"You know? The government. He's also hiding from the Care Bears, I think."

"How do you know all this?"

"He gave me a pamphlet about it." She whistles. "Scary stuff. At least in his mind. Don't worry. He's harmless."

I nod, though I'm still super confused. The bus rumbles and the doors close. No turning back now. I'm stuck on this bus with Marty and Steve and whoever is wearing that massive cowboy hat.

"So who's this person you're going to see, and why do they need your help?" Marty asks.

"She's just someone I know," I say, hoping Marty will leave it at that. I already know she will most certainly not leave it at that.

Marty narrows her eyes at me. "*How* do you know her?"

"I know her...online."

Marty's mouth drops open so wide that I can see a silver filling in one of her back molars, which kind of makes me feel better because her teeth aren't completely perfect. "You're going to help someone you met *online*? Are you serious?"

63

"Yeah." I shrug. "Kids these days, right?"

"Wrong," Marty snaps. "You do realize it could be someone else posing as a little girl. A *predator*, Jolene. Hasn't anyone ever taught you not to talk to strangers online?"

"It's not a predator," I insist.

"But what if it is? What if it's some guy in Australia trying to lure you there to be some kind of child bride?"

"Does that happen?"

Marty stares at me seriously. "I couldn't say for certain that it *doesn't* happen."

I roll my eyes. "I guess if he's in Australia then I'm pretty safe. I couldn't afford a plane ticket anyway."

"He'd probably be willing to pay his new wife's way."

"There's no Australian." I huff. "I've tried explaining this to a hundred people already, but no one will listen. I know it's a girl because I've seen her a bunch of times on video. She does a live-streamed show where she flies this ultralight trike."

"She flies a trike? Like a tricycle? You're going to help a girl who does a show on a flying tricycle?"

"No, it's like a plane with three wheels. I guess that's why it's called a trike."

"This twelve-year-old girl flies a *plane*?"

"Not a real plane. It's a glider thing with a propeller. Anyone can fly them. You don't need a license or anything."

"That's pretty cool." She grins. "I should get one. I can picture myself pulling up to school in that."

"Yeah," I say. "It is pretty cool. Except she crashed it."

"Whoa."

"And I'm the only one who saw it." It's such a relief to tell Marty this that I slump down in my seat, letting all my breath out. This feels different from when I told the others—like she's really listening right now.

"Why don't you call the police?"

"I tried. I don't know her real name or anything, so they're not taking it seriously."

"What about your friend's parents?"

"I don't know who they are. And her mom doesn't even know she flies the ultralight."

Marty sits there, blinking and thinking, like maybe she can figure this out for me. "And your parents?" she asks.

I shrug. "My mom's not any help either."

"Does she know what you're doing?"

"I let her know." And that is the truth.

"So she gave you permission? She was like"—Marty raises her voice to a high-pitched squeak—"'Why, yes, Jolene, my sweet young child. Please go off into the dangerous unknown all by yourself and save this dear girl you only know online. I'll make pot roast while you're gone.'"

"My mom doesn't make pot roast."

Marty stares at me. "What did she say, then?"

"She said it's okay."

Marty crosses her arms. "Why don't I believe you?"

I throw my hands in the air. "She said it's okay. Okay? She's really busy with other stuff right now, and she doesn't care what I do. All she cares about is—" I stop.

"What?"

"Nothing." I can't believe I almost just said that. I almost said *getting her pills*.

"Oh, no. Now you have to tell me."

I suck in a breath. "It's nothing. She...she has this friend who's taking a lot of pills and so she's dealing with that—helping her friend."

Marty stares at me like she has X-ray vision and is trying to see the truth in my head. "What *kind* of pills?"

"You're awfully nosy, aren't you?"

"I totally am. What kind of pills are they? Does your mom know? Did she tell you? What do they look like? Do they have letters or numbers on them?"

"I think it's oxycodone," I say softly, but I don't *think* anything. I *know* they're oxycodone. Sometimes hydrocodone. Sometimes they have other names, but they're all the same thing. I've looked up all the letters and numbers on them at the library.

Marty grimaces. "Oh, jeez. I'm sorry. Your mom's friend must be an addict."

I turn away from Marty and stare at my reflection in the bus window. I've never allowed myself to say the word before. *Addict.* Like if I never said it, I could stop it all before it got too bad. But I've known for a long time.

Tears well up in my eyes, but I blink them away. Crying never helped anything get better in my life. All it ever did was cause the kids at school to call me a crybaby, and I am *not* a crybaby. They can call me Snaggletooth and White Fang and Homeless Jo, but I won't give them a reason to call me crybaby.

When I'm certain my eyes are dry, I turn back to Marty. "Can her friend get better?"

She shrugs. "If she wants to."

"What if she doesn't? What if she doesn't think she's an...addict?"

"Then she'll keep taking them. She'll need more and more all the time because you build up a tolerance. One day she'll take so much that she dies."

"Jeez!" I say. "Why'd you have to jump straight to death?"

"Sorry if that upset you, but it's the truth. Lots of people die from that stuff."

"How do you know so much about it?"

Marty draws her eyebrows together and pushes a hand through her blue-streaked hair. "I just do. It's, like, common knowledge these days. Kids at my school even take and sell oxy."

"I've done some research myself," I say. "If my mom can get her friend into a drug treatment center—"

Marty cuts me off. "You can't force her to go. She has to choose to go." Then she squints at me. "Why are you so concerned about your mom's friend?"

"What do you mean?"

"Why are you doing research about drug treatment centers and all that? I thought your mom was the one helping her. Why is it so important to you?"

I shake my head. "I don't want to talk about this anymore."

"Why not?"

"I just don't," I say, trying to keep calm. To

change the subject, I ask, "What do you think will be the best way to get to Alamo Lake from Quartzsite?"

"Wait." Marty holds up a hand, her many bracelets jangling together, glinting under the small overhead light. "You're trying to get out to Alamo Lake? And hold on a second. What about the person who's supposed to be picking you up?"

"Um, I'm sure they'll be there, but in case they're not—"

"You are totally lying."

"Okay, fine," I say. "None of that matters. I have to get to Alamo Lake. I know exactly where Addie crashed. I need to go to the Flipside Café and then walk only about three miles. Maybe a little farther. That's it."

"You've got to be kidding me. Why are you on a bus to Quartzsite?"

"There's no bus to Alamo Lake or even Wenden. This was the closest I could get. Do you think a taxi will be the best way?"

Marty scoffs. "A taxi? In Quartzsite? At ten o'clock at night? Have you ever been to Quartzsite?"

I shake my head. The truth is I've never been anywhere outside Phoenix before, but I don't want Marty to know that.

She snorts. "There's nothing there. Seriously. It's just a bunch of old people with their RVs." Marty stares at me in complete seriousness. "It is, without a doubt, the most boring place on earth."

"I'll figure it out." But my nausea is getting worse.

Marty raises an eyebrow. "It's like a hundred miles to Alamo Lake from Quartzsite. A hundred miles, Jolene. In the middle of the desert. In the middle of the night." She narrows her eyes to slits. *One hundred miles.*

"It's actually more like eighty." I slam my head back against the headrest. "There's got to be some way to get to the Flipside Café from Quartzsite."

"And if there's not, what will you do?"

"I'll find a way."

"But what if there's not?"

"Will you stop saying that? There has to be a way."

Marty shakes her head. "You, Jolene, are experiencing a little thing we call denial."

"I know she's out there alone and hurt. She could be dying, and I can't get anyone else to go. What would you do if it was your friend in trouble?"

"If it was *my* friend, she would not go out in the desert at all. It's dangerous."

"Like I said"—I glare at Marty—"I don't have any choice."

"But why is it up to you?"

"Because no one else will help me," I snap. "It's up to me because no one else will help me." Story of my life. "Anyway, I'll be fine. I have supplies."

"What kind of supplies?"

Marty gestures for my backpack, and I let her pick through the pathetic food inside. As though on cue, my stomach growls.

Marty glowers. "This isn't enough. When was the last time you ate?"

"I ate right before I left," I lie. "A huge meal." I hold my arms out as wide as I can between the black vinyl seats. "Absolutely huge."

"You're lying."

Darn it. How can she always tell? "Fine. I had a bowl of Cheerios this morning."

"You can't do this on a bowl of Cheerios."

"All I'm doing is sitting. And I'll eat a big meal at the Flipside. A huge meal—absolutely gigantic."

"They won't be open in the middle of the night. Your plan has more holes than your tennis shoes, which, by the way, are not exactly the optimal sort of shoe for hiking in the desert, even if they didn't look fifty years old."

I stare down at my shoes. "They're all I have."

Marty's face softens. "It's going to be really hot, Jolene."

"I have a lot of water." I pull the gallon jug out of my backpack.

"What if it's not enough?"

"It will be." I shake the jug, and the water sloshes. "It's a whole gallon."

"What if you get hurt?"

"I won't. I know the area."

"How do you know the area? Have you been there?"

"No, but I've mapped it. And I've seen it on Addie's show. There are trails. It's an easy walk."

Marty glances at the window, then back at me,

then around the bus, then back at me. "I feel like . . .
I should stop you."

"No!" I hadn't meant to say it so loudly, and a few
sleepy-looking people turn their heads toward us.

Marty smiles at them. "We're fine. She's fine."

Suddenly, the jittery white guy gets up and
walks down the aisle. He leans on Marty's seat.
Marty looks so furious that it almost makes me
burst out laughing.

"Hi, girls. What are you up to tonight?" he asks,
scratching at his blotchy, stubbly neck.

"Move along, sir!" Marty says with a booming
voice that surprises even me. The guy jumps a little
before scurrying away to the bathroom, where I'm
pretty sure he's going to have to fight Steve if he
wants in. "Creeper," Marty whispers.

But I'm glaring at her now. "You can't stop me,"
I hiss. "I've come all this way."

"You have much farther to go."

"It's night. I won't get too hot. It will be okay."

Marty looks like she's agonizing over what to
do. She eventually shakes her head. "Let's just call
the police right now."

"I told you I did that!"

"Then maybe she's already been found."

"I told you they didn't take it seriously. Do you think they'll take you seriously?"

Marty shrugs. "I guess not. Still, maybe some-one has found her. She could be at the hospital. Why don't we call the hospitals around Alamo Lake tonight to see if she's been brought in?"

I want to scream. "I don't know her real name. How are they supposed to tell us if she was brought in when I don't even know her name?"

"When we get to Grandpa's, we'll figure it out."

I kick the empty seat in front of me and huff. And while we waste time figuring things out, Addie could be out in the desert dying. I can't let that happen.

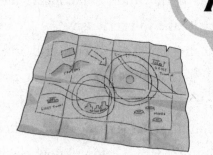

# 20 DAYS AGO

## BLIPSTREAM DIRECT MESSENGER

**Addie Earhart:** So I looked up tacophile, and it turns out it's not actually a real word. I think it should be, but I haven't figured out who I have to petition to get it into the dictionary. What are you doing? And will you sign my petition to make tacophile a real word?

**JoJo12:** Yes, I'll sign your petition. I'm just hanging out at the library. What are you doing?

**Addie Earhart:** Nothing. Bored. Boredom is the worst. I can't stop thinking about how bad I miss my dad.

**JoJo12:** Where is he?

**Addie Earhart:** He died. Six months ago. Car accident.

**JoJo12:** Oh my gosh. Me and my mom were in a bad car accident a couple of years ago.

**Addie Earhart:** Did you get hurt?

**JoJo12:** Not too bad, but my mom got really hurt.

**Addie Earhart:** Is she OK now?

**JoJo12:** She hasn't been the same since the car accident. She's tired and sick and sad a lot. We used to be closer. I'm so sorry about your dad. You must miss him a lot.

**Addie Earhart:** Yeah. I do. I better go.

**JoJo12:** OK. Sorry if I made you sad.

**Addie Earhart:** You didn't. I mean, I am sad, but it's not your fault.

**JoJo12:** Sorry. I'll see you later, Aviator.

**Addie Earhart:** After a while, bibliophile. That really is a real word, and it means someone who loves books, and you said you like travel books.

**JoJo12:** It's good 😊

# NOW

It's barely past ten o'clock by the time we reach Quartzsite, and I've been sitting here sulking next to Marty. Who does she think she is to stop me? I knew this would happen. I knew that if anyone else got involved, they would mess it up.

The bus reaches our stop, and we both stand and stretch before hobbling down the aisle with the other groggy passengers. For a moment at the door I think maybe I can make a run for it, but I suspect Marty will easily chase me down. Her legs are way longer than mine.

Marty points in one direction. "His trailer park is only a few blocks from here. We have to walk it."

I glance down the dark road and then back at the brightly lit bus stop. "I have to go to the bathroom," I say.

Marty scrunches up her nose. "You don't need to use the nasty bus stop bathroom. We're only a few minutes from my grandpa's."

I cross my legs and bounce like a toddler. "I have to go *bad*," I whine.

Marty narrows her eyes at me. "I know what you're doing. No way, Jolene." She grasps my arm and pulls me along. She doesn't let go for a long time, like she thinks I might bolt at any second. She's totally right. That's all I can think about. I am scheming, positively *scheming*, about how I'm going to get out of here and get to Addie. Could I use some kind of decoy? All I have is my water and snacks. Maybe I could open the sardines and make her pass out from the smell. Or throw a handful of cracker crumbs in her eyes.

I wish Marty would understand that we're wasting precious time. At the very least we should be running to her grandpa's trailer. I know she means well and wants to help. And she *did* protect us from the creepers on the bus, so I feel like I can trust her, but she's not taking this seriously enough.

We walk through the front entrance of the trailer park and pass a bunch of colorful metal cactuses and lizards cluttering the small yards. One tiny lawn still displays an old plastic nativity scene left over from

Christmas. Actually, by the look of it, all cracked and sun faded, it probably stays up year-round.

We reach Marty's grandpa's trailer, and she pulls out a set of keys to let us in. The smell of warm garbage hits me as we walk through the door. "Whoa," Marty says, setting the keys on the messy kitchen counter. "Looks like I got here just in time." The kitchen sink overflows with dishes, and the garbage can is piled high with empty microwave dinner boxes. Flies buzz around my head as Marty picks up an old phone that has actual buttons and a curly cord. I wonder if she's calling the hospital, but then she says, "Hi, Dad. I made it okay."

When she hangs up, I expect her to help me with a rescue plan, but instead she empties the stinking trash, setting the bag on the front porch. Then she grabs a fly swatter from the wall and starts chasing the flies down.

I haven't removed my backpack or sat down, nor do I plan to. "Um," I say, clearing my throat. "Excuse me, but we need to figure out what to do about Addie. Maybe your grandpa can get up and drive us out there."

Marty stops mid-swat and stares at me. "He can't do that."

I fold my arms. "Why not?"

"He's asleep, Jolene. And even if he was awake, he definitely can't handle driving all the way to Alamo Lake in the middle of the night."

"Then why did you bring me here in the first place?"

"I brought you here to keep you from wandering out in the desert by yourself. And to feed you and make you get some sleep. Then we'll deal with it in the morning. There's nothing that can be done right now."

I throw my head back and breathe, the car-crash feeling getting worse by the second. "It's late now. Addie's mom would've already come home from work and found her gone. Maybe she's called the police."

"Okay," Marty says, back to swatting flies.

"So we should call them and see if they'll tell us if anyone has reported a missing child."

"I don't even know if they'll tell us that information. You said they didn't take you seriously."

"Well, you sound older than me, so you should call them and find out. It's worth trying."

Marty slams the fly swatter on the coffee table. "Got him!" Then she looks at me, breathing hard from her fly massacre. "Okay." She picks up the old phone. "Grandpa doesn't have a cell phone. No internet or computer either, so you need to look up the number for me. Unless you want to wait while I use the *phone book*."

"Of course," I mutter, plugging my phone into an outlet in the kitchen to make sure it's charged for whenever I'm able to escape this trailer park prison. Then I look up the number.

Marty dials, and I listen intently as she talks to the person on the line. She gives her name and information, and I'm glad she's using such a mature adult voice. Then she asks, "Has anyone reported a missing child in this area?"

Pacing across the tiny living room, I wish I could hear the other person. I wonder if it's the same man I spoke to earlier. I assume the person is asking why Marty wants this information and if she has something to report because Marty says, "Well, I suspect that a child *may* have gone missing."

I wish she hadn't put so much emphasis on the word *may*.

"Yes," she continues. "I know a kid who went out near the Alamo Lake area. She was flying a plane—"

"Ultralight," I say.

"Right, ultralight," Marty corrects. "We think she may have crashed earlier today."

There's that word again: *may*.

Marty nods her head a few times. "Uh-huh," she says. Then she sighs. "Yeah, sorry we don't know her name."

"Her name is Addie," I say quickly. "Tell them Addie."

"We think her name is Addie," Marty says. Then she listens, nodding more and rubbing her forehead. "Yeah, sorry—no last name. It's kind of complicated. She was livestreaming a video online when she crashed. Maybe you could send someone out to the area to look around?"

Marty glances at me while she continues listening,

and I can tell whatever is being said isn't great. Finally she says, "Thank you so much for your help. We'll call if we're able to get any more information." She places the phone back on its base.

"So what did they say?" I ask.

Marty picks up a dirty bowl and puts it in the kitchen sink. "Well, they're going to look at any missing child reports to see if one could be Addie. They're also going to call the ranger out at Alamo Lake, but they said he might not respond until morning. Then they'll go out there tomorrow and take a look around."

So basically, almost all the things the man told me earlier, except this time they said they'd take a look. "She's not close to any road," I say. "They won't see her. They need to fly someone out there."

"Jolene," Marty says, leaning against the kitchen counter and rubbing her eyes. "It's expensive to send helicopters out. They're not going to do that without solid evidence and information. I seriously doubt they'll even send a car at this point." Then her eyes widen and she startles a bit, like she just realized what she said. "I'm sure they'll send one first thing in the morning, though," she adds quickly.

It's so obvious she doesn't believe that at all. She probably still doesn't even believe *me*. She's just like everyone else. "Liar!" I yell.

She shushes me and says, "You're going to wake my grandpa up."

"You know they're not going to do anything, and even if they go out there tomorrow, it could be too late. Addie needs help *now*. I know it. What if she's bleeding to death?"

"Listen," Marty says. "You need to let this go, Jolene. You can't do anything about it."

I knew it. She just wants me to forget about the whole thing. "I can get out there right now!"

"How?"

I pick my phone back up. "I'm calling an Uber."

Marty shakes her head. "There are no Ubers in Quartzsite at this time of night. I doubt you could even get one in the middle of the day. Jeez, Jolene. Haven't you ever been outside the city before?"

I ignore her, opening up the Uber app I installed and entering the Flipside Café as my destination.

The little circle whirls and whirls, searching for a car. But Marty's right.

"See?" she says. "I'm not trying to lie to you, Jolene."

"That's fine," I insist. "I'll find another bus."

"You know as well as I do that no bus goes to Alamo Lake."

"I'll walk!"

"Eighty miles?"

"So? I can do it."

"You couldn't even get there by morning. I doubt you could walk there in two days. Plus, you would probably die."

"Emma Gatewood walked the whole Appalachian Trail when she was seventy-five years old," I say. "That's over two thousand miles."

"Who's Emma Gatewood?"

"An old lady!"

"I'm pretty sure the Appalachian Trail isn't over a hundred degrees."

"Let's take your grandpa's car. I saw it out front."

"I told you I can't drive without an adult."

"Addie might die," I tell her, fighting the tears

back. No way am I crying in front of Marty. I have to stay strong.

Marty's face softens, and she tilts her head. "She might not even be out there," she says gently.

I shake my head, clench my fists. "You're wrong. She's out there." Despite my best efforts, a tear breaks loose.

Marty walks over and hugs me. "It's going to be okay, Jolene."

"No, it's not." I sniff, my arms limp at my sides, my fists still clenched. I rub my nose on Marty's shoulder, hoping I leave a snot smear.

"Maybe it would help if you called your mom," she says. "It might make you feel better."

But I can't call Mom because I have her phone. And she can only call me if she leaves the apartment and asks someone for help.

When I don't say anything, Marty pulls away. "C'mon, let's eat something and get some sleep. Things will look better in the morning."

"Okay," I say, nodding and wiping my nose. I force a smile, covering my mouth. "Let's eat and sleep." But there's no way I'm staying in this trailer all night.

## 8

MARTY PULLS OUT THE SLEEPER SOFA AND GRABS SOME blankets from a cabinet after we've eaten a couple of microwave dinners—Swedish meatballs for Marty and Salisbury steak for me. I've never eaten Salisbury steak before, and it's pretty good.

I check my phone to see how the battery's doing, wishing it would charge faster since I'll be leaving the moment Marty's asleep. As I open BlipStream messenger, my pulse speeds up. I bet the car-crash feeling would dissolve away if I got something back from Addie:

*I'm okay!*

*They found me!*

*I'm in the hospital!*

And then what? Then I'd get on a bus back to Phoenix and go home. To what? All the same stuff. Because nothing ever changes. Would Mom even know that I had ever been gone? It would almost be like it never happened at all. Well, until she got the credit card bill with my bus ticket on it. But there aren't any messages from Addie, so I slip my shoes off and climb onto the sofa bed with Marty.

"I'm sorry I don't have any pajamas for you," Marty says. "I only brought one pair for myself."

"That's okay," I say, and it is definitely okay. Changing out of pajamas would just be one more obstacle to my escape.

Marty switches off the lamp, and we lie in bed, side-by-side, the blanket pulled up to our chins, despite how warm it is in the trailer. "Hey, Jolene," she says.

"Yeah?" I mumble, trying to sound like I'm half-asleep already.

"Does your mom really have a friend who takes oxycodone?"

I swallow, wondering why she would ask me that. "Yes."

Marty rolls onto her side, and I can feel her staring at me in the dim glow of a nearby night-light. "You can talk to me," she says. "If there's anything going on at home you want to tell me, I'll understand. I really will. More than you know."

I feel my eyes well up, and I hope it's too dark for Marty to see. What a crybaby I am.

"Keeping secrets doesn't always help people," she says. "Sometimes you need to tell the truth to help them."

I want to tell Marty the truth, but then I remember what happened to Benjamin. And I remember Aunt Mallory. I can't trust what Marty might do if she knew. She already wouldn't listen to me about Addie.

"There's nothing to tell," I say. "Everything's great at home."

Marty's quiet awhile. "Okay," she finally says. "But if you ever want to tell me anything, I'll listen. I...I know what it feels like to want to run away from everything."

"I'm not running away." The last thing I need is for Marty to suspect that I'm some kind of runaway and report me.

"I just want you to know you can trust me. I won't..."

But she doesn't finish whatever she was about to say. And I don't ask. I want her to go to sleep, and not just so I can sneak out. I don't like these questions. Marty should mind her own business.

"Why is this Addie thing so important to you?" she asks, instead of whatever she was going to say.

My throat suddenly feels as dry as the desert, and I struggle to swallow. "Addie's my friend," I whisper, staring up at the dark ceiling, at the fan lazily whirling above us. "And I don't have many friends."

I can feel Marty watching me for a minute until she finally rolls onto her other side. "Good night," she says softly, and I suddenly have this horrible homesickness feeling on top of the car-crash feeling. Combined, it makes me want to flip over and scream and sob into my pillow, like that's the only way I might be able to get it all out. But I can't afford to do that, so I put it all in another box and store it away deep inside.

My eyes feel heavy as I wait for Marty's breathing to change, but I absolutely cannot allow myself to fall asleep. At one point, I gently poke her, and she groggily says, "What?"

"Oh, sorry," I say. "Nothing. Sometimes I poke people in my sleep. Like sleepwalking, but sleep... poking."

"That's a first," she mumbles. "I hope it doesn't go on all night." But a few minutes later, she's snoring softly.

The old sofa sleeper creaks nonstop as I try to pull the blanket down and get out of the bed as quietly as possible. I keep glancing at Marty, but she continues snoring. I grab my old sneakers and pull my phone off the charger. Then I take the charger out of the outlet, wincing when it makes a cracking sound.

The sleeper sofa is close to the front door, so I wander down the dark hallway, hoping to escape through a back door. I startle to a stop when I hear a loud noise, but it's just Marty's grandpa, snoring like Marty. I spot a door and carefully unlock and step through it onto some rickety wooden steps. Closing the door softly behind me, I make a run for freedom. For Addie.

## 9

# 16 DAYS AGO

## BLIPSTREAM DIRECT MESSENGER

**JoJo12:** Guess what? I got a book about Amelia Earhart. It's interesting. What do you think happened to her?

**Addie Earhart:** She's living happily on some island somewhere, surviving on coconuts and fish.

**JoJo12:** All this time? This books says she was born in 1897. Wouldn't she be pretty old?

**Addie Earhart:** Like 120, but coconuts and fish are very healthy.

**JoJo12:** Is she your favorite aviator?

**Addie Earhart:** Close, but no. My favorite is Bessie Coleman. Queen Bess!

**JoJo12:** Why is she your favorite?

**Addie Earhart:** She had to learn French just so she could go to France to get her pilot's license because Black women weren't allowed to do that here. Then she became a barnstormer! Nothing could stop her!

**JoJo12:** What happened to her?

**Addie Earhart:** She died in a plane crash.

**JoJo12:** It seems like being a pilot's really dangerous. First Amelia Earhart and now Queen Bess.

**Addie Earhart:** Yeah, but they didn't let fear or people or anything else stop them from doing what they wanted. And neither will I! One day I'll fly over the ocean just like Amelia.

**JoJo12:** I guess I can understand wanting to fly away.

**Addie Earhart:** You know, the ultralight does have two seats.

**Addie Earhart:** Hint, hint 😉

**JoJo12:** You'd have to pick me up in Phoenix.

**Addie Earhart:** No problem! My ultralight can fly anywhere.

**JoJo12:** Do you think it can make it to Paris?

**Addie Earhart:** Paris is officially on the itinerary.

**JoJo12:** Egypt?

**Addie Earhart:** Also added.

**JoJo12:** Then I'll see you later, Aviator.

**Addie Earhart:** After a while, JoJo-Pile.

**Addie Earhart:** Of Awesomeness.

# NOW

I'm walking along an empty road in Quartzsite, just outside Marty's grandpa's trailer park. I'm definitely relieved to have escaped, but I also have to admit I have no good plan. I am totally planless. I am completely and absolutely without any kind of plan. I bet Valentina Tereshkova didn't fly into space without a plan. I bet she wasn't like, *Hey, guys! No worries! I'll figure out how to get to space once I get in that rocket. Haven't you guys ever heard of winging it?*

I am definitely winging it here. And part of winging it apparently includes sneaking into Rovin' Roads RV Campground, which is what I'm now doing, to see if I can find a bicycle or something since I still can't get an Uber or taxi or bus. I'd even settle for a camel. Robyn Davidson crossed the Australian desert with camels, and she did it all alone. If I'm able to find a bike, it will be way faster than walking and definitely less stinky than a camel. Plus, a bike won't spit at me or buck me off. I hope.

Sweat drips down my back. I swipe my hair away from my sticky neck and pull it into a ponytail. How can it still be this hot at midnight? I bet it's ninety degrees.

I try to figure out how long it will take me to get to Alamo Lake if I can ride a bike ten miles per hour. I'm not great at math, but I can divide eighty miles by ten. Eight hours. That would put me at Alamo Lake by about eight in the morning. It won't be so blazing hot yet, and I can still get to Addie before the hottest part of the day.

I walk past the front office of the campground. It's dark and empty, and there doesn't seem to be anything like a security guard. I wander past motor homes and travel trailers—big ones, small ones, silver ones, and old ones that stink so much I can smell them even outside. I pass by so many motor homes without any sign of a bike that I would seriously be willing to settle for a unicycle at this point. I wonder if I could ride a unicycle.

Finally, I stop at a big fancy RV. I want to jump up and down and shout, but I don't because I'll wake up the old people. The RV has a bicycle tied to the back, but it's not just a regular bicycle—it has a *motor* on it. I have hit the mother lode.

But am I really going to steal? I've never stolen before. Yeah, I took Mom's phone and credit card, but I'm really only borrowing them. I didn't steal them. Is it okay to steal if it's for a good reason? I mean, if a person is starving and they steal a can of food, is that wrong? I don't think so. And isn't this basically the same thing? Stealing to save someone?

I shift from foot to foot, debating and agonizing

over what to do. And then I have an idea. I throw my backpack down and pull out my notebook and pencil and begin writing under a nearby streetlamp.

Dear Motorbike Owner,

I want you to know I borrowed (NOT stole) your motorbike or whatever it's called. Please understand that it was for a good cause. A desperate cause! My friend is in serious life-threatening trouble, crashed, injured, possibly dying out in the desert, and I have to do whatever it takes to reach her. I was nearly about to give up all hope until I found your motorbike thingy. Now I feel hope again! I promise to return it. If you don't have it back by tomorrow, please call me at the phone number I've included, and I'll tell you how to get your bike back or maybe I can find a way to bring it to you. Anyway, the important thing is that you'll definitely be getting it back, so please don't call the police. Again, I'm so very sorry, but this was a matter of life and death. Thank

you for your honorable sacrifice. Please know
it was used to save a life.

   Signed,

   The Mysterious Motorbike BORROWER

   (not thief)

## 10

I DON'T WANT TO RISK WAKING PEOPLE BY STARTING THE bike up inside the RV park, so I walk it quietly down the road. I stop to study it, my only light the gloomy glow of the crescent moon. Too bad it's not a full moon tonight.

How in the world do I get this thing turned on? There's no ignition or key, no pull start like a lawn-mower, no buttons of any kind. I try to get on the bike, but my butt can't reach the seat even when I hop up and down. I find a latch on the post, open it, and then push the seat down as far as it will go. Then I refasten the latch and jump back on, my butt barely reaching the seat as I stand on tiptoe. I grip the rubber handles, turning them like a motor-cycle game I once played at a pizza place. The right one turns, but nothing happens.

I jump off the bike and gape at it, throwing my hands up in frustration. I want to kick the stupid tires, but I'm not going to risk breaking it somehow. Well, it's a bike, after all, and I'll just have to ride it like a bike. I swing a leg over the top, kick up the kickstand, and start moving down the road in a standing position since sitting on the seat makes pedaling difficult. I wish the bike's owner weren't so tall.

What a complete waste. The motor would be so much quicker. My legs feel heavy and are already cramping after only a few minutes. I find myself overwhelmingly exhausted at the thought of riding this bike eighty miles to Alamo Lake, especially as I get closer to the freeway, guided by the head-lights of the giant semitrucks barreling by, one after another.

I pedal down the dark road hoping to avoid the busy freeway as long as possible. I know I'll have to get on it at some point, though, because it's the only way to Wenden. I checked and double-checked the online map, hoping for some other way, but there's none, unless I want to ride through the desert, which would be a bad idea. One large cactus needle in the wrong place and I'd have a flat tire.

I won't have to be on the freeway for very long, but the loud whooshing and humming of the semis gives me the car-crash feeling. I'll ride on the shoulder, of course, as far away from the drivers as possible. But what if a big truck doesn't see me? What if a sleepy driver veers a little?

My lips are already dry, my mouth parched. I'm thirsty, but this part of my journey has barely begun, and I have eighty miles to go. I'll have to save my water as long as possible. Gripping the rubber handles until my hands sting, I twist the right one a little. It turns and a motor sound suddenly roars, making my heart leap into my throat. My sweaty hands slip from the handlebars, causing me to swerve across the road and nearly wipe out in the dirt.

Squeezing the brakes, I stick out a leg to catch myself, then stand, straddling the center bar of the bike, looking around, breathing hard, my body vibrating. Did the sound come from another car? No one else is on this road.

That motor sound came from *me*. Of course—I have to be *moving* to start the bike. Heart pounding, I stand on the pedals again. As soon as the bike is really moving, I twist the right handle. The motor roars as before, then sputters. I have to twist back on it half a dozen times before the motor fully comes to life.

"Yes!" I cry into the dark desert. Now I just have to figure out how to drive the darn thing. I twist back on the handle and the bike speeds up, nearly jolting me off. I release the handle and it slows down. No problem.

Now that the bike is working, I stop and allow myself a few small sips of water to wet my dry mouth. The eighty miles will be much easier now, but I still don't want to be too greedy with so far to go. I put my water back in my pack and continue on, twisting back on the handle more gently this time. Wiping out would be bad news, especially since I'm not wearing a helmet or pads or anything protective whatsoever. Plus, I can barely tell where the road and shoulder divide. For a second, an image of me skidding across the dark pavement comes to mind. I can see my shredded bare arms and legs, skinned knees, bloody elbows.

I'll have to be extra careful—not too fast. And even though I'm going pretty slow, it's still way faster than pedaling. I imagine I'm Lois Pryce as I enter the on-ramp, staying on the shoulder as far away from the cars as possible without ending up in the desert. Lois Pryce rode a motorcycle from Alaska all the way to the very tip of Argentina, the length of two whole continents. The little bit of time I'll be on this freeway isn't even close to that. If Lois Pryce can do what she did, then I can do this, too. Probably.

There aren't any big streetlights, but enough cars zoom by to help me keep track of the road. The first semi that passes nearly stops my heart when it honks its booming horn, blasting me with the hot night air. I wobble on the shoulder, concentrating with all my might on keeping the bike steady.

The next semi swerves to the side close to me,

so close that it hits the "drunk bumps," as Mom used to call them when we drove places. The drunk bumps are ridges built into the road along the sides that make loud vibrating noises when vehicles hit them. That way the driver knows they're veering too far off the road, and if they've fallen asleep, it should wake them up.

The semi passes, and the hum of the drunk bumps fades. It's quiet a moment, and I think again about Lois Pryce, wondering if she ever felt this light-headed, if her hands ever got this sweaty, if she ever gasped for air. She was probably brave all the time, unlike me.

I'm imagining Lois Pryce soaring over a snowy Alaskan mountain pass, steep cliffs at every turn, when another semi comes up behind me. I swerve as far away from it as I can, but the bike starts wobbling. One second I'm on the seat, and then I'm not. My body slams against the road, knocking the air out of my lungs. Stars burst in my eyes, and then I'm rolling across the hot blacktop, still unable to breathe or stop myself. I stretch my arms out and the gritty asphalt tears my palms and elbows.

When I'm finally still, I lie on the ground, desperate for air to fill my burning lungs, absolutely frozen by the thought that I might be injured and this is the end of my journey. The loud hum of another semi fills my ears. Don't they ever stop?

Finally finding my breath, I move a little, something digging into my back. The road is all lumpy, and a realization grips me. I'm not lying on rocks or gravel. The lumpiness under my back is the drunk bumps.

Another semi is coming, and half my body is in the road.

## 11

THE RUMBLING OF THE SEMI BUILDS, MAKING THE ROAD under me vibrate like an earthquake. The tremors attack my head and back and limbs, gluing me to the ground. My body has been so fully taken over by the car-crash feeling, it's like I'm back there in the car, and the old brown truck is about to hit me. Only this time it's a great big semi.

Before it's too late, I manage to force myself to roll off the drunk bumps. Pain shoots from my knees through the rest of my legs when I crawl farther out of the path of the semi just as it passes. I don't stop crawling until the asphalt ends.

I sit at the edge of the shoulder, nearly in the desert, and hug my bloodied legs, waiting for my body to stop quaking. And then the semi screeches to a stop way ahead of me. I hold my breath, listening in the dark as a door slams shut. "Hello? Are you okay?" a man calls. When another car drives by, I see his silhouette—big and bulky and moving toward me.

I don't waste any more time. Shooting to my feet, I frantically run along the shoulder, looking for the bike. I spot it about twenty feet away, and I'm shocked at how far I rolled. I grab the bike and jump on, hoping it didn't get damaged during my crash. It seems okay, so I start pedaling. There's no going backward. I have to pedal past the truck driver and hope he doesn't chase me down.

"Hey!" he calls as I race toward him, pulling back on the handle with my torn, stinging hands. "Hey! Hold up!" The man waves his arms frantically. "Stop!"

But I don't. This man could be dangerous. Or maybe he'll call the police. Either way, I absolutely can't stop. The motor comes to life, flooding my shaky body with relief that it still works. The man leaps out of my way in surprise when I zoom past him, blood and wind rushing in my ears, the buzz of the bike's motor drowning out his cries. I see the off-ramp for Wenden up ahead. Almost there. Thank goodness I'm almost there.

I veer off and down the ramp, which fortunately comes just before the man's stopped semi, so he won't be able to follow me. The traffic now behind me, I enter the blackness of the desert highway. With nothing but the crescent moon overhead, I can barely see the road or shoulder or desert surrounding me while my eyes adjust to this new level of darkness. But I still don't stop until the freeway is totally out of sight.

I finally squeeze the brakes, my whole body quivering from my ordeal. I lift one weak, shaking leg off and put the kickstand down. The silence pushes in on me from all around. The dark feels suffocating as I breathe in and out, waiting for my pulse to slow. I feel wetness on my butt. Was I so scared that I *peed* myself? Gross!

And then it hits me. "No!" I cry out to the

darkness, tearing my backpack off and unzipping it with trembling hands. I pull out the gallon jug of water, which is now smashed from when I struck the ground. The force of the fall popped the lid off, and most of the water has spilled out into my backpack, soaking everything inside.

And I had been saving it for my long journey. My heart sinks all the way to my worn sneakers. I'm already thirsty. I should've drunk more when I had the chance. And then something else occurs to me.

Ripping open the small front pocket of the backpack, I take the phone out and push the power button. The screen lights up. I let out a huge sigh of relief and slip the phone into the back pocket of my shorts. Then I pull out my map and hold it up. It's damp, and I can hear the water drip, drip, dripping, against the pavement. I hold the map over my head and let the water drizzle into my mouth, not wanting to waste another drop. I assure myself that pencil doesn't bleed. It will dry. It will be okay. I'll still be able to read it. At least, I think so.

I dig through the backpack, pulling out the

soggy bread and crackers and tossing them on the ground. I use the phone's flashlight to see how much water is left in my jug—maybe a few sips at best. A cracking sound startles me, and I turn in a circle, shining the flashlight into the darkness, finding nothing but trees and cactuses. No homes or buildings or stores or anything. The flashlight drains the phone's battery, so I move to turn it off, but then a pair of glowing eyes reflects back at me from the desert. I jump, holding in my scream before the eyes disappear, the creature now hidden behind the brush.

Even though I'm terrified of whatever's out there, I turn the flashlight off to save the battery. Now it's just me and the mystery animal, which I hope is a deer and not a wolf. Are there deer or wolves in the desert? Maybe it's a chupacabra. What even *is* a chupacabra? I only know it's something scary.

I try to focus. It's about thirty miles to get to Wenden, and I have almost no water left. But it's dark and I have the motorbike, which means, even though it's still hot, I don't have to wear myself out with pedaling and get even thirstier. I can still do this.

Now that I'm starting to calm down, the pain is returning. I hold my throbbing palms in front my face, but I can't see much of anything except for some dark smears across my white skin. I put the nearly empty container back in my backpack and then place the wet map gently on top of it, hoping it doesn't tear.

My skinned knee stings as I bend my leg to get on the bike. I'm tempted to take the phone back out and use the flashlight to inspect my injuries, but I'm scared to know how badly I'm scraped up. It won't matter anyway, so I start pedaling, my knees burning with the motion.

Not a single car has passed by since I left the freeway, so I decide it's safest to ride in the center of the road, as far away as possible from the slim shoulder, where there may be gravel. If a car does come, the headlights will give me plenty of warning.

After about a minute, I twist back on the handle, my palms burning, and start the bike up. With so little light, it's as though I'm gliding through ink.

All it would take is one rabbit or lizard or rock, and I could wipe out again. As I squeeze the handlebars, my palms and fingers pulse.

The Van Buren sisters rode motorcycles across the entire United States—thousands and thousands of miles. I only have to go about eighty miles. I bet the Van Buren sisters were never this scared on their whole trip. Of course, they *did* have each other. I know it's best that I do this all on my own, but it would be kind of nice to have someone else with me, to *not* be so alone. Marty suddenly pops into my mind, and I squeeze the handlebars even tighter.

I remind myself of Bessie Stringfield, the first Black woman to ride a motorcycle solo across the United States. She rode her own Harley during World War II, delivering important mail to army bases. And she had to deal with people attacking her all the time and telling her she shouldn't even be *allowed* to ride a motorcycle. Just because she was Black.

But no matter how much I think about those brave women, my insides stay all knotted up, and

I still feel guilty when I think of Marty waking up and finding me gone. Still wish someone else were here with me, though I can't think of any specific person, which makes me wish I had a real someone to wish for. Benjamin was a real someone for me at one time.

The road suddenly starts feeling extra bumpy, and the bike slows. I stop, put the kickstand down, and get off. I pinch the front tire and it feels okay. But then I pinch the back tire—flat.

I breathe in deep, run my sore hands through my hair and grip it hard at the scalp. Standing in the dark in the middle of the road, breathing and thinking, I pull out my messy loose ponytail and redo it. Then I box up the car-crash feeling and store it away. I've collected a lot of boxes on this trip, probably more than I ever have before. And I can feel every single one of them stacked inside, wobbling and swaying and about to topple at any moment.

The ride will be extra bumpy now, but I'll have to deal with it. After all, the motor will still run, even with a flat tire, so I get back on the bike and pedal, pedal, pedal, twisting the handle. The motor sputters and dies. I pedal with all my strength, twisting the handle over and over again, until sweat drips down my temples. But the motor keeps sputtering and dying.

There's no way I can build enough speed to start the motor now. By stopping and checking the tire, I basically ensured I wouldn't be able to get the motor going again. Or maybe it died along with the flat tire. With the way my luck's been going, anything is possible.

With the flat tire, pedaling is exhausting. I twist the handle back every now and then to check, just in case, but it's no use. It's getting harder to pedal, and the ride is getting bumpier all the time. The tire feels like it's coming apart, and soon I'll be riding on the rim. I can't keep this up. All this work and sweat is making me thirsty, and only those few sips of water are left.

I stop and jump off the bike, pushing it along the dark road, ready to abandon it behind a bush somewhere, when a light appears in the distance.

Is a car coming? No, it doesn't seem to be moving. More lights come into view, and I feel a burst of excitement. It's a town. Finally. But it's too soon to be Wenden. This must be Hope.

As I push the bike toward the town, my pace picks up. Maybe there will be something, anything, there. I stop and pull out my phone to check my location on the map. It's Hope, which has a gas station, and gas stations are always open twenty-four hours. I'll be able to charge my phone and maybe even get a new tire or maybe they'll have that stuff you spray into the tire to keep it from going flat. Everything is going to work out. Everything is going to be fine. This whole winging it thing is turning out great.

Practically skipping, I near Hope, but my excitement begins to fade the closer I get. It's very quiet, and not a single car is driving around. How could there be so few cars anywhere in the whole world? I continue pushing the bike down the street until I reach the gas station. The *dark* gas station. Putting the kickstand down, I leave the bike in the small parking lot to peer into the windows. Totally dark outside. Totally dark inside. I knock on the window, even though it's obvious no one's there. But gas stations are open twenty-four hours!

Marty's words echo in my mind, like she's right here next to me still acting like my mom. *Haven't you ever been outside the city before?*

What do I do now? Try to call for a car again? It's worth a shot, even if this place is smaller than Quartzsite. You never know. Maybe my luck will change. I open the Uber app and enter my destination. The spinning wheel tells me all I need to know, and I don't want to waste more battery life searching for a car that will never come.

If I'm going to walk to Wenden from here, I'd better get going.

Three minutes. That's how long it takes me to walk through this whole town. What would it take to walk through Phoenix? Three *days*? How could I be so stupid to think that everything would be like it is in Phoenix, that just because there's a town where a few people live, there have to be twenty-four-hour gas stations and taxis and restaurants and stores?

I hide the bike in some bushes under a big sign where the town ends so I'll be able to tell the owner exactly where it is. Then I look at the sign: YOU'RE NOW BEYOND HOPE.

"No kidding," I grumble, kicking the dirt and making my way out to the dark desert on foot.

## 12

I'M WALKING IN THE DARK IN THE MIDDLE OF THE HIGHWAY
in the middle of the night in the middle of nowhere.
I'm not even worried about a car coming anymore.
How could any place on earth be this dead?

One comfort in all this deadness is the stars,
which I can barely see in Phoenix. I had no idea
they could look like this. It's like the whole sky is
on fire, though I wish the fire would give me a little
more light down here on the ground.

I check my phone after a while to see how far
I've gotten. I stop and gape at the map. One mile?
How could it only be one mile since I left Hope? It
feels like ten. But even more shocking is that my

phone is back down to 2 percent. It will never make it the next eleven miles to Wenden. I put the phone away and take a deep breath.

It's a straight shot on this road. I won't need the map, and I'll be able to charge my battery once I get there. Even if I have to sit on the gas station floor and wait, that's fine. I'll do what I have to do.

With nothing but the dark desert to keep me company, my mind starts wandering to all kinds of things I don't like to think about—the same things that bug me when I wake up in the middle of the night and can't go back to sleep. Funny. It's probably about the same time right now as when that always happens.

Of course I think about Addie. Is she okay? Is she thirsty? Does she have her water or did she lose it in the crash? If she lost her water, then I don't see how she could…What am I going to find out there? Will there be blood? Will I be able to handle it? I remember how I thought Mom was dead right after the car accident. It was so scary. Her not waking up. And the blood. So much blood.

*Don't think about that, Jolene.*

Instead I think about Benjamin, wondering where he is and what he's doing, remembering this one time at school when some kids called me Snaggletooth, and Benjamin told them to stop. They pushed him and called him a loser. Afterward, I told him he didn't have to stick up for me like that. It didn't help, and then he just got bullied, too. He told me he was still happy he did it.

Thinking about him makes my heart ache. Is he with a nice foster family? Does he go to a school where the kids aren't mean to him? Does he have enough to eat? I really hope so.

I think about Marty, still sleeping in her grandpa's trailer. Will she be mad at me when she wakes up? I would definitely say yes to that question. She'll probably wish she'd never met me. She'll probably be relieved that I'm gone and that she won't have to deal with me anymore.

My mind circles back to Mom, her words popping into my head: *I have enough to deal with right now.* I don't want to think about her. Because if I start thinking about her, I'll drive myself totally bonkers. And yet.

Is she worried about me? Does she wonder how I'm doing? Does she even suspect at all what a hard time I'm having? Will she take more pills tomorrow? Will she take so many she dies?

Are any of these people thinking about *me* right now?

I pull out my phone to check where I am, but it won't turn on. Who knows how much farther I have to go now. It could be two more miles or ten more miles. My legs tell me it must only be two more miles, but my mind knows it's probably much farther still.

Every inch of my skin burns from wiping out on the bike, and my feet ache in my too-tight sneakers. I can feel every rock in the road through soles as thin as paper. My whole body hurts. I take out the water jug and tilt my head back, allowing the last little bit of water to trickle into my mouth.

Then I freeze in the darkness, the jug in front of my face. Something is making a faint noise, though I can't see what it is. The sound gets louder.

Having lived in the city my whole life, I really don't know a whole lot about what's out here in the desert. I've learned about animals at school, of course, and I even went on a field trip once to the zoo, which had a whole Arizona section. But there's only one animal that could possibly make a sound like this—a buzzing that gets louder then dimmer, louder then dimmer. I heard it on Addie's show. A rattlesnake.

A rattlesnake I can't see.

Addie said rattlesnakes can strike at a distance two-thirds their body length, so I need to stay that far away from it. But I don't know where it is or how long it is or even what two-thirds of any number is because I'm terrible at fractions.

So I just stand here, totally frozen, my heart drumming, my body trembling. If my phone weren't dead, I could use its flashlight. Should I stay still or should I move? Does it have night vision? Or can it sense my heat? I have no idea what to do except stare at the ground, hoping some kind of movement, or the lighter coloring of the snake against the dark asphalt, might jump out at me. But I can't see anything at all. I decide to take one cautious step. The buzzing gets louder. My heart beats so hard that it feels like it might tear right through my chest.

And then I see movement out the corner of my

eye to the left. I inch away in the other direction, then run down the middle of the road until the buzzing fades before slowing down to a walk, hoping my breathing will slow down, too.

What would I have done if the snake had bitten me? I couldn't call for help. There are no cars to flag down. Nowhere to run, except all the way back to Hope, where I might be able to wake someone up. But that's a long way away.

I know what would have happened if it had bitten me. I'd have keeled over on my way back to Hope. Just keeled over dead. Based on the number of cars I've seen, it might have been several days before someone even found my body. By then, it would have been eaten by animals and buzzards and stuff. Or maybe it would never be found out here. Maybe I'd disappear without a trace, like Amelia Earhart. Maybe like Addie.

*Stop it, Jolene. That is not going to happen.*

The truth is, anything could be hiding in this darkness. As much as I've longed for adventures, I always knew they would be too dangerous. But this barely even qualifies as an adventure. Just a three-hour drive. That's all it was supposed to be. No big deal. It's not like I'm climbing mountains or boating down hundreds of miles of dangerous river or crossing the Arctic or mapping places no one has ever seen before. There won't be any drowning or freezing or falling off mountains.

But still, how could a three-hour drive have turned into all this? And I'm still so very far from Addie. I add up all the miles in my mind. Maybe ten more miles to Wenden plus another thirty to the Flipside Café and then about three miles into the desert to find Addie. Forty-three miles.

But Sarah Marquis walked ten thousand miles. Ten. Thousand. Miles. What is forty-three compared to ten thousand? I just have to concentrate on the mile in front of me. I'm sure that's what Sarah Marquis did. It's not like she was saying to herself, *Only nine thousand nine hundred and fifty-two more miles to go, Sarah.* No, she probably took it one mile at a time.

I concentrate on watching the ground, listening for any more rattlesnakes. As long as I don't get bitten by one, it will be okay. I'll be okay.

And then someone screams. I freeze and listen, fear gripping my whole body. Yes, it's screaming— way off in the distance someone is screaming. I bolt, all worries about rattlesnakes totally gone.

What is it? What could it possibly be? It sounds like zombies. More screaming, and I'm running blindly in the dark, the car-crash feeling pushing me into total panic, the screams getting louder, and oh my gosh, I'm running right for it, aren't I? I'm running right into the mouths of the zombies.

I stop, panting, body shaking so hard I might shake to pieces. I sit down in the middle of the road, hugging my scraped knees, burying my head in them as the screaming gets clearer and turns into anguished howls and crying.

It's people being tortured. Or zombies. Or people being tortured and eaten by zombies!

*Please go away.*

*Please leave me alone.*

*Please don't eat me.*

Too terrified to even lift my head from my knees, I murmur my pleas. Amid all the howls and screams and the blood pulsing in my ears, I'm finally able to make out a noise that sounds like a bark. And then more barking and whooping and yelping.

It's dogs. No, not dogs. Coyotes.

Coyotes are better than zombies, but still. I can't fight them off. Coyotes are a kind of dog, right? And dogs are really good at hearing and smelling. Can they hear me? Smell me?

Benjamin had a dog, and he said that dogs could read our minds. So I send a message out to the coyotes with my mind: *I'm skin and bones. No meat here. Not even enough for an appetizer.*

I hear a light clacking—nails on road. I squeeze my knees in tighter. Something is panting, and it's not me. I try to hold my breath, but I'm already suffocating, gasping for every bit of air, as I breathe hard into my knees.

*Clack, clack, clack.*

I fight the scream in my throat.

*Sniff, sniff.*

I squeeze my knees. I don't want to die like this. I still have to find Addie. And I know that if I die here right now, Addie will surely die, too.

## 13

JUST WHEN I THINK I WON'T BE ABLE TO STAY QUIET another second, the clacking sound starts moving away. The howling and yipping and screaming start to peter out, too.

And now it's completely quiet again except for the thumping in my head. It takes me a while to pry my stiff arms off my knees, and even longer to find the strength to stand on rubbery legs. I turn in a circle.

They're gone. Thank goodness, they're gone. But which direction was I going? Which direction did I come from?

Darkness surrounds me as I turn in circles,

searching for anything to signal the right direction. I look up at the bright stars. Explorers frequently use the stars to guide their way, but I didn't think to do that, didn't think I could possibly lose my way on a straight road.

What about the moon? It was a little behind me, right? I mean, what's the worst that could happen? If I go in the wrong direction, I'll end up back in Hope. Then I would have to turn around and come back this way. How many extra miles would that add to this already endless walk? And how could I be so incredibly stupid?

I can't stand here all night. Following my instincts, I move forward with the moon at my back. My legs feel like they've been pummeled by and then filled with bricks. I don't know how much longer I can keep going. I push myself forward, thinking of Addie with every step. Unlike me, Addie wouldn't be scared. She would be brave. She would keep going. She wouldn't give up or stop.

I keep dragging my feet over the pavement. It feels like forever since the coyotes. I still haven't found myself back in Hope, so I think I'm moving in the right direction. I make sure to keep track of the moon so I don't get disoriented again.

My legs start to give out just as I spot a few lights in the distance. Wenden. Finally. I've made it nearly the whole twelve miles. Seeing those lights, knowing I'm almost there, gives me the final burst of energy to make the last mile.

*Addie, I'm coming. I'll be there soon.*

The lights are two streetlamps illuminating the completely empty road. I hobble by a few quiet trailers with KEEP OUT and BEWARE OF DOG signs on chain-link fences before finding the gas station. It looks dead like everything else around here, but it has to be open soon, even if it isn't open twenty-four hours. It will have to open early in the morning, and I can wait.

But the Wenden gas station isn't open. It will never be open, no matter what time it is. The windows are boarded up, the paint peeling, the pumps gone. An old spigot juts out from one cracked wall, and I turn it, hoping for water. But there's none. I circle the building looking for an outlet to charge my phone. Again there's none. No water. No charging. No anything. I might as well be stranded on an island like Amelia Earhart.

A CONDEMNED notice is stapled to the front door. I can read it easily, even the small print, and I realize the sky is starting to brighten. It's morning. I walked all night long.

Thirty-three more miles to go.

An old splintered wooden bench still stands bolted to the cracked pavement next to the front door. I pull my backpack off, lie down on the bench on my side with the bag under my head like a pillow, hug my bent legs, and cry myself to sleep in the early light of the hot morning.

# 14

## 14 DAYS AGO

### BLIPSTREAM DIRECT MESSENGER

**JoJo12:** I dreamed we were flying the ultralight together last night. We were really going on our trip.

**Addie Earhart:** Cool! I dreamed my dog turned into one of those scooter cart things at the grocery store and I was riding him around, but he still had his whole head even though his body was the scooter, and his head kept eating all the food off the shelves as we drove around, and then we got kicked out of the grocery store.

**JoJo12:** You spend a lot of time at the grocery store, don't you?

**Addie Earhart:** I told you THERE'S NOTHING ELSE TO DO HERE! Plus they have good donuts. The blueberry fritter is my favorite.

**JoJo12:** I like chocolate with sprinkles. You have a dog?

**Addie Earhart:** Yeah! Haven't I ever told you about him? He's a golden retriever. His name is the Fluffinator of Fluff Nation, but we call him Nate for short. Do you have a dog?

**JoJo12:** No. My mom says we have to have a yard before we can have a dog. Plus apartments always charge extra if you have a pet. Do you have a backyard?

**Addie Earhart:** Yeah. And a front one too. So where were we going in your dream?

**JoJo12:** I don't know. The only thing that mattered was that we were going. I wish it could really happen.

**Addie Earhart:** It will happen! We're going to Egypt, remember?

**JoJo12:** Right 😊

# NOW

I startle awake, pushing myself up on the rickety bench. I forget where I am for a moment, then I hear loud honking.

An old station wagon idles in the parking lot right in front of me. The grimy window rolls down, all jerky and creaking, and a head appears—a head with lots of piercings and blond, blue-streaked hair.

Marty clucks her tongue. "You little sneak."

I'm feeling so many things right now at seeing her—relief, annoyance, shame, curiosity. Did she really drive here without her grandpa? How did she find me? What exactly is her plan in coming here? My head spins with questions and hunger and thirst and confusion. Every inch of my body aches, I suppose from wiping out on the bike. And sleeping on the hard wooden slats of the bench. And walking all those miles.

I stay on the bench, digging my shoes into the cracked pavement and folding my arms, making it clear that I will not be going with her this time. She'll have to drag my limp body into the car, and even as strong as she is, I'm not sure she can manage that.

"What are you doing here?" I ask.

She gapes at me. "Well, let's see. I was just a little bit worried when I woke up early this morning and found that you had snuck out like some kind of criminal. And it looks like I was right to worry."

"I'm not a criminal," I snap. "I had every right to leave. You can't hold me hostage. And I'm doing fine. You can go home."

She takes a deep breath, and her face softens. "If you think I'm leaving you here on a bench in the middle of nowhere when you look like you're already half-dead, then you're more cracker pants than I realized."

"You're cracker pants if you think I'm going home with you." I'm not totally sure that cracker pants is actually a thing, but if it is, I'm definitely not it.

Marty shakes her head. "I'm not taking you home with me, Jolene."

"Then why are you here?"

"It's pretty obvious I can't stop you. You'll

probably just run away again. But I can't let you make the trip alone." She leans her head back against the headrest and sighs, looking up at the car ceiling, her arms straight out in front of her, both hands gripping the steering wheel. "So against all my better judgment and wisdom and intelligence— which is vast by the way, quite vast—I'm going with you."

I study her, my eyes narrowed. "You're lying. If I get in that car, you'll take me back. Then I'll lose all the progress I've made."

She lifts her backpack from the seat and opens it to the window. "Look, I'm not lying. I even brought supplies. See, there are some hard-boiled eggs, prunes, and Ensure." She bites her lip like she's trying not to smile.

"What's Ensure?" I ask suspiciously.

She looks like she's holding back a laugh. "It's like a milkshake for old people."

I stand up from the bench and hobble over, my legs stiff and stinging. I cover my mouth and giggle a little. "What kind of supplies are these?"

She fully laughs now. "I know, right? It's all my

grandpa had unless you wanted me to bring some more microwave dinners. And he doesn't have anything as fancy as a *water bottle*, so I had to clean out a jar of salsa and fill it."

I grab the jar of water from her and greedily gulp about half of it down.

Marty raises an eyebrow. "Thirsty, huh?"

I wipe my mouth and nod. "Most of my water spilled last night."

She nods like she somehow already knew this. Or expected it. "Please get in," she says. "I promise I won't take you back."

Should I trust her? I'm still not sure. Maybe the old-person supplies are a trick. But as I look down the road toward Alamo Lake, the weight of the remaining thirty miles crushes me. It's already getting hot. In a few hours, it will be unbearable. For both me and Addie. Plus, I need Marty's water. I really don't see another choice.

I walk around the car, getting in on the passenger side. The smell of the station wagon immediately takes me back to Mom's and my old car. It had the same exact smell of super-old car that's been sitting in the Arizona sun.

"How'd you get scraped up so badly?" Marty asks once the car gets moving.

I look down at my bloodied knees. "I had an accident."

"An accident?"

"Yeah, I...uh. I wiped out on a bike."

"What bike?"

"I borrowed a bike from someone at this RV park because I couldn't get a car."

Marty raises an eyebrow. "Borrowed?"

I turn my full body toward her. "Yes, borrowed. I left a note and everything with my phone number so I can give it back to them."

"Well then, where is it?"

"It got a flat tire, so I had to leave it hidden somewhere." Marty is giving me a very disapproving look, so I add, "I will be able to tell them exactly where to find it, so you see, I didn't steal it. I really did borrow it."

"If you say so," Marty mumbles.

I clear my throat. "What did you tell your grandpa?"

She shrugs. "Nothing. He was still asleep, so I just left."

"Won't he get worried about you?"

"I'm hoping he doesn't know I was ever there, that he thinks I didn't come. I'm sure this won't take very long. It's only a few miles out into the desert from the Flipside. So let's see..." Marty lifts one finger at a time off the steering wheel, counting. "A half hour to drive there. Then an hour to get out to the spot where you think Addie crashed. Then another hour to walk back and then a half hour to drive home." She smiles. "We'll probably be back before he even wakes up."

"You're leaving out all the time we'll need to get Addie some help."

She nods quickly. "Right," she says, and I can tell she still doesn't believe anyone is really out there. "If Addie's there, she'll be able to give us all her information. Then we can call her parents."

"Parent," I say. "Addie only has a mom. Like

me. But what if your grandpa calls your parents or they call him?"

"I'll deal with it if I have to." She shrugs. "Oh, and you wouldn't believe what I had to do to find you. Check this out." She reaches into the back seat, one hand on the wheel, and grabs a giant, crinkled map that hits me in the face as she pulls it into the front with us. "This is what's called a *map*, Jolene. I'm pretty sure they stopped making them in the eighteen hundreds, but old people still have them."

I giggle and cover my mouth. "I actually know a lot about maps," I tell her. "I like drawing them. I have a detailed one of Alamo Lake we can use when we get there." I open my backpack and remove my damp map, spreading it out carefully so it can dry on the drive.

Marty glances from the road to my map and back. "Wow, that's good, Jolene. You really do like making maps, don't you?"

"Of course," I say.

"It's just kind of an odd hobby for a little kid."

"I'm not a little kid." Sheesh. How many times

do I have to remind her of this fact? "I like to imagine all the places I would go if I could."

"You mean if you weren't a little kid?" She snickers.

I roll my eyes, and she pushes my arm lightly. "I'm just messing with you," she says. "Where do you want to go?"

"No, now I'm not telling you."

"Please? Pretty please?"

I shake my head and cross my arms. "Nope."

"Okay, let me guess." She scratches her cheek. "You want to go to Wales for the Elvis Festival."

I burst out laughing. "That's not a real thing."

"Yes, it is. I read about it in a magazine. Okay, let me take another guess. You want to go to...to Kansas to see the world's largest ball of twine."

I roll my eyes again. "I want to see a lot more than Kansas."

"Sounds like you need to choose a career that allows you to travel."

"Like what?"

"Maybe a flight attendant," says Marty. "Or a software sales guy. My dad has a friend who sells software, and he has to drive to Tucson every other *week*. There's good stuff to see in Tucson." Marty taps her blue fingernails on the steering wheel. "Lots of good stuff in Tucson."

"I want to travel a lot farther than Tucson."

"Well, where then?"

"Like Paris, to see the Louvre and the Eiffel Tower. And Africa to see the Sahara Desert. And Alaska and Argentina and all over the place."

"Then you need a most awesome job, like someone who works for a travel magazine or something like that. You know, taking pictures or writing articles. Oh! Maybe writing *and* illustrating articles, since you're so good at drawing."

I run a finger slowly over my map, along Addie's most recent route. "I doubt that could ever happen."

"Why not?"

I concentrate on the winding road in front of us that cuts through endless desert—rocky mountain slopes dotted with hundreds of saguaros and ocotillos jutting up from the ground like small geysers. I blink away the forming tears, not wanting Marty to see. "Poor people can't do stuff like that."

Marty shakes her head. "Cuss that, Jolene. That's some messed-up thinking. Yeah, everything might be harder, and nothing will be handed to you like people who get to go to fancy private schools and have cussing college funds and Teslas with a big fat red cussing bow in the driveway when they turn sixteen, but that doesn't mean it's impossible."

I can tell she's getting worked up based on the number of times she's said the word *cuss*. I think about this trip. Just a three-hour drive. How much easier would all this have been if I had...more than what I have?

"Anyway," Marty says. "Whatever you accomplish, it will mean even more. Because you did it yourself. *You* did it. Even though it was really hard." She draws in a deep breath. "Your life is full of possibilities." But she seems to be talking more to herself than to me—like she has to convince herself, too. "Endless possibilities," she adds in a whisper.

"Endless possibilities take endless money," I say.

She smiles. "Or endless determination."

The ride gets bumpy as the road turns to dirt, and I ask her, "So what are you going to do, then?"

Marty slows the car down, and her face grows serious. "I'm going to be a doctor, and I'm going to help people." She glances away from the dirt road for a second to look at me. "People like your mom's *friend*." She says *friend* in a funny way, like maybe this friend I've made up is made up. Looking back at the road, she says, "And by doing that, maybe I can help people like you. People who are...kind of like me." A muscle twitches in her jaw like she's clenching her teeth. "No one should have to go through that."

I stare at her. "What do you mean?" But before Marty can explain, the car makes a strange lurching motion. "What was that?" I ask.

Marty leans forward and looks at the dash. "I don't know."

The car begins making all these sputtering noises, jerking, then stalling. Marty grips the steering wheel, the muscles on her arms bulging. "It. Won't. Turn," she forces out.

I reach over and pull on the wheel so she can steer it to the side of the dirt road. We finally come to a stop, and the car lets out a loud popping noise. I jump and cover my ears.

"That's just a backfire," says Marty, breathing hard.

"What happened?" I ask. "Are we broken down?"

Marty's still grabbing the steering wheel, and she presses her forehead to it. "No, no, no," she says. "I'm not even allowed to drive by myself. My parents are going to kill me."

"Why?" I ask. "What's wrong?"

She faces me, her head still resting against the steering wheel. "We're out of gas."

## 15

"PLEASE TELL ME YOU'RE KIDDING," I SAY.

Marty throws her hands up. "Hey! I'm sorry I didn't think to go fill up when I was rushing frantically out the door to save your bony butt!"

"My bony butt did not need saving! And how could you not think about gas?"

"You'd still be sleeping at the gas station if it weren't for me," Marty says. "So yes, your bony butt did, in fact, need saving. You should be grateful—you *are* a lot closer now."

"Yeah, but now we have to walk the rest of the way."

"Still better than walking thirty miles." Then

her eyes get big. "How much farther is it, do you think?"

I pull out my map and try to identify any kind of landmark nearby. I spot a large rocky cliff with a hole cut into it that looks like a window. "Not far. Maybe a mile."

We grab our backpacks and start walking. Marty throws her head back and groans. "This sucks! It's so stinking hot already." She kicks the dirt. "This is way too much heat for you after being up all night. How about you stay at the Flipside when we get there, and I go see what I can find?"

"No way!"

"Why not? I can find Addie using your map."

"There are a hundred reasons why not."

"Give me one."

"I know the area better."

Marty snorts. "You've never even been here."

"No, but I've watched Addie's show a lot, and I know it from that. Plus, I drew the map."

"I can figure it out."

I huff. I know Marty is totally capable. Clearly she is. So what's the problem? How can I tell Marty that I need to be the one who finds Addie? After I've come all this way, I need to be the one who finds her. And maybe not just for Addie.

"Fine," she says. "I guess I can't expect you to stay back after all you've gone through. I just worry about you getting sick and passing out in the desert or something. And then what will I do? I don't want to have to drag you out."

"That's not going to happen."

"I've heard of people dying on even shorter walks in the desert. Like a few years ago, there were these people who died on a walk in Encanto Park. They were just walking around on the sidewalk and fell over dead from heatstroke. Like this." Marty lets her head fall to the side and sticks her tongue out. "Instant deadness."

"That so did not happen," I say, laughing.

"Maybe it was Saguaro National Park," she says. "Close enough anyway."

"Encanto Park is hardly Saguaro National Park."

"You're right. This desert we're about to go into is much more similar." Then we walk quietly for a little while until Marty asks, "Have you talked to your mom?"

I study the bright dirt in my path, which makes my tired eyes ache. I swing my backpack around and take out Mom's old sunglasses and slip them on. They're foggy, cracked, and scratched, but they help with the glare. "No, but my phone's been dead since the middle of the night," I say.

Marty pulls out the salsa jar of water and takes a swig before handing it to me. "You can charge your phone and call her at the café. I'm sure she's worried about you."

I take the jar. "Maybe."

"You know," Marty says. "Sometimes people do stuff or act in ways that make it seem like they don't care about us. But that doesn't mean they don't."

I scowl at the ground, taking small sips of water. It tastes like salsa water. "What do you know about it?" I say, with a little more bitterness than I intended.

Marty sighs. "It just seems like you don't like to talk about your mom much, and maybe that means something."

I kick at a rock. "Why do you have to be so nosy?" I mutter.

"Why do you have to be so secretive?"

I don't respond to Marty's last question as we make our way around a curve, spotting some buildings in the distance. "There they are," I say instead. "We're almost there." I look way off in the direction where I think Addie might be and see a span of reddish cliffside and a large mountain jutting up like a massive pyramid, pointed at the top.

We trudge quietly along the hot dirt road toward the Flipside Café, and I notice a landing strip in the distance with a small plane parked near it. A tall pole stands at one end of the landing strip, an orange triangular flag fluttering in the hot breeze at its top, and I wonder if Addie has ever been there.

As though Marty read my thoughts, she says, "I wonder if that's where your cracker pants friend takes off in her flying tricycle."

I snort. "She's not cracker pants, whatever that even means."

Marty raises an eyebrow. "Oh, you know what it means."

I think of Addie flying the ultralight and live-streaming her show. I remember how close she's gotten to scorpions, even picking one up. I remember her trying to chase down the wild pig, standing so close to the rattlesnake, and even swimming in the lake in her clothes because she saw a pelican.

Addie's just really brave. And maybe a *tiny* bit cracker pants.

## 16

# 12 DAYS AGO

## BLIPSTREAM DIRECT MESSENGER

**Addie Earhart:** I sent Joanie Cash a letter and she wrote me back!

**JoJo12:** Who's that?

**Addie Earhart:** She was one of the first commercial airline pilots who's an actual WOMAN. She said she's very impressed that I already know how to fly the ultralight, but she wants me to be careful. And she says I can totally be a pilot when I grow up.

**JoJo12:** Do you have to go to college for that?

**Addie Earhart:** No. But you have to have a lot of flight time—like over a thousand hours. And you have to take some hard tests.

**JoJo12:** You'll do it. You're smart. You have a good left brain, remember?

**Addie Earhart:** You're smart, too! What do you want to do?

**JoJo12:** I don't know. I'll never be able to go to college or anything like that.

**Addie Earhart:** There are lots of things you can do without going to college. Like being a pilot!

**JoJo12:** Not when you don't have any money. How would I get flight time? And I'm sure I won't go to a good high school.

**Addie Earhart:** Stop being so down on yourself! You can do all kinds of things.

**JoJo12:** I'm just being realistic.

**Addie Earhart:** No. You're being a Negative Nancy. A Debbie Downer. A Pessimistic Patty!

**JoJo12:** Why are these all girl names?

**Addie Earhart:** Ew. You're right. Let's make up some new ones. Gloomy Gary!

**JoJo12:** Hopeless Harry!

**Addie Earhart:** Bleak Barry!

**JoJo12:** 😄

# NOW

"I cannot believe how hot it is already," Marty says, wiping sweat from her face. We've already finished off the water in the salsa jar.

I'm careful not to agree with her. "It's not that bad." I shrug, even though my whole back is soaking wet against my backpack, and my temples are pulsating.

She gives me the side-eye. "Liar."

I am definitely lying, of course. It's hotter than a bonfire, but I can't say or do anything that will give Marty a reason to keep us from heading into the desert. "No, it's really nice out actually," I say. "Not nearly as bad as I thought it would be."

Marty shakes her head as we pass through an open metal gate. A sign near the entrance reads, DRIVE SLOWLY, LIZARD XING. We walk through a small RV park, past several palm trees, to a wooden building with a big front porch topped by an old metal roof. About half a dozen heat-battered picnic tables stand out front.

I spot the OPEN sign in the window and feel suddenly relieved. I hadn't even thought to check if the café would be open. With the way things have been going, I wouldn't have been surprised if it was permanently closed.

"Good thing they're open this early," Marty says.

We walk up the wooden stairs of the porch and step inside the café. I push my sunglasses on top of my head so I can see. Unlike the outside, the café's inside is anything but plain—colorful metal signs and license plates and neon words cover the walls, which are literally wallpapered in dollar bills. Hundreds of men's ties hang from the ceiling.

"Well, good morning, girls," an older woman with short, curly gray hair says from behind the counter.

"Good morning," says Marty.

"Where on earth did you two come from?" the woman asks.

I glance at Marty, hoping she has some kind of good story to tell. I'm still not used to this lying thing, and making stuff up on the spot is hard.

As I hoped, Marty takes charge. "Just drove in for breakfast. Our grandpa says you have the best breakfast within a hundred miles."

I can't help but think there probably isn't another restaurant within a hundred miles.

The woman smiles. "Oh, isn't that nice. Who's your grandpa?"

"His name's Martin," says Marty.

"Hm." The woman scratches her head. "Can't say I know a Martin, but then again I don't know everyone's name who comes in here, of course." The woman points to my bloodied knees. "You get in some kind of accident, honey?"

"Skateboarding," Marty says, rolling her eyes. "Too bad she's not very good at it."

I scowl at Marty. "Am too," I say.

"Aren't you a tough little thing?" the woman

says, motioning for us to sit. We throw our bags down and sit on a couple of old metal barstools in the middle of the counter. The woman brings us some water, and we chug it until the ice rattles.

"Thirsty, huh?" The woman slaps two greasy plastic menus down in front of us. "Y'all sisters?"

Marty slams her glass down and puts an arm around me. "Yep. This is my little sister, Bertha."

I elbow her. "Knock it off, *Olga*."

The woman raises an eyebrow. "Y'all got some old-fashioned names." She smiles. "I like it. My name's Ellie."

"Nice to meet you, Ellie," Marty says, picking up her menu and scanning it.

Two people are eating breakfast at opposite ends of the counter—an older man, who's totally ignoring us, and another older woman, who's watching us with curiosity. It seems everyone in this part of the state is old.

"Can I charge my phone, please, um, Ellie?" I ask.

"Of course." Ellie grabs our water glasses and

refills them in the sink behind the bar. "There's an outlet right under your feet."

I dig out my phone and charger and plug them in. Then I hit the power button repeatedly until it finally has enough life to turn back on. I go straight to my BlipStream messages, but there's nothing.

Marty looks up from her menu. "Anything new?"

I shake my head and place the phone down, the disappointment replacing any hunger I'd been feeling with nausea. Nothing looks good on the menu. I really want to get out of here, but I know I should eat, and the phone needs time to charge anyway. I feel someone's eyes on me and peek over my menu to see the old woman at the counter staring. She lifts a piece of toast to her mouth and takes a bite, chewing thoughtfully, still watching me. She seems vaguely familiar, but I can't imagine why. "You two live nearby?" she asks.

I look at Marty, and she says, "We live in Quartzsite."

"That's awfully far to come for breakfast," the woman says. "What's that? Fifty miles?"

"Eighty," I say, feeling each of those eighty miles in every inch of my skin and bones and muscles.

"We needed a girls' day out together," says Marty. "Where are you from?" she asks the woman. It's amazing how easily Marty talks to people.

"Wickenburg."

"That's as far as Quartzsite, isn't it?" Marty asks. "You staying here at the RV park?"

The woman shakes her head, taking another bite of toast. "Nope. I just came in for breakfast. Like you two."

I look around the café and spot the restrooms. "I think I need to use the bathroom," I say, jumping down from the barstool and grabbing my bag. "I'll be right back." I hurry to the bathroom and shut the door. Pennies are scattered across the floor. I squat down to touch one, but it's stuck, glued down. Dollar bills for wallpaper. Pennies for flooring. Just...why?

*Lily loves Gavin* is written on one of the dollars, and I notice that they all have something written on them—customers have actually stapled the dollars to the walls. If I had a dollar, I would never staple

160

it to some wall for no good reason. I peel the dollar back and see another dollar behind it. I peel that one back and find yet another dollar. The dollar bills are at least three layers thick and cover every wall in the whole café. That must be thousands of dollars. *Thousands.* Probably enough for a car and new clothes. Maybe even enough for a drug treatment center. And it's just sitting here on these walls doing nothing. Completely wasted.

I take the jug out of my backpack and fill it in the sink. I didn't want to ask Ellie to do it in case it made her suspicious. I also wash my hands and splash my face with water, which feels ice cold against my hot skin and gives me the chills. Then I check myself out in a mirror framed by horseshoes— the first time I've really looked at myself in forever. Dark rings sag under my eyes. My hair is all greasy and stringy, barely in its ponytail. My skin is red and dry. I'm embarrassed to go back and sit in the café now that I know how I look.

My stomach cramps a little, and I feel like I might have to vomit. There isn't much in there *to* vomit, except the Salisbury steak from the night before. I hope I'm not getting sick. Probably just tired and overheated, but if I am getting sick, Marty definitely can't find out.

When the cramping eases, I redo my ponytail and head back out to the counter, where Marty squints at me. "I was about to come check on you," she says. "I thought maybe you'd escaped out the bathroom window."

I jut my chin out. "It was too small."

She smiles and shakes her head.

"I filled my water," I whisper to her. Then I pick up the phone and check the battery life. "It's only up to six percent. Why's it taking so long?"

"Young people these days are obsessed with those things," the old woman at the counter says before Marty can answer.

Marty and I both look at the woman, but we don't say anything. Marty whispers to me, "It will be okay. We only need a couple of hours of battery life."

But I'm not sure it will be okay. Every part of me is jittery and jumpy and screaming to leave, to get to Addie, to get out of here and into the desert.

It's getting hotter and hotter outside, and I can't believe we're stuck here because of the stupid phone battery.

I stand back up and walk around the café after we order our food, hoping it will relieve the jumpy feeling. Lots of pictures hang on the dollar-bill walls. They must be photos of the surrounding area. I even recognize some spots—the mud canyon, ghost towns, and mines.

Then I find something really exciting—a giant map of the whole Alamo Lake area. It's far more detailed than anything I've found before. Unlike the maps I've been using online and at the library, it has pins all over the place with little sticky notes attached that tell you exactly what's there. I'll be able to find even more landmarks to guide our way to Addie. I run to my backpack and pull out my map and pencil.

"What's up?" Marty asks.

"There's a great map on the wall over there," I tell her. "I'm going to make some changes." I run back to the map, taking a moment to lean against the wall until a wave of dizziness passes, reassuring myself I'll feel better after I drink more water and eat something. Once the restaurant stops wobbling, I make a few corrections to my map.

Suddenly I feel someone behind me. I turn and find that nosy old woman again. "Did you draw that map?" she asks.

"Yes," I say, making some notes. Addie will be in a wash, right at a bend. I clearly see the trail that leads to the wash after the mud canyon. If we follow that trail, then follow the wash, we should run right into Addie without having to trek through thick desert.

"Your map is very good," the woman says. "You're quite the cartographer."

"Thank you."

"They teaching you kids that sort of thing in school now?"

My hand freezes. I swallow. "No. My mom taught me. She's really good at drawing."

"Bertha, your breakfast is ready," Ellie calls from the bar, and it takes me a minute to realize she's talking to me. I quickly fold the map and walk back to the counter, sitting down in front of my oatmeal, my stomach churning at the sight of it. Before forcing my first bite down, I check my phone again—12 percent.

"See? Obsessed," that old woman says behind me. "Put your time into your drawing instead of that phone, and I think you'll do all right. You've got some artistic talent there."

I look at Marty, who's grinning. "I'm going to the bathroom," she says. "I'll be right back."

I shove another bite of oatmeal into my mouth. This one's not as hard to get down.

"Well, I'm off," the nosy old woman says to Ellie. "Delicious as always, my dear."

"Thanks for coming in, Joanie," Ellie says. "Always good to see you. Fly safe."

I whirl around on my barstool to take another look at the woman.

"You keep drawing those maps," she tells me, picking up a leather bag from next to her stool. Then she turns and walks out the door, letting a whoosh of hot air into the café.

I whip back around to face Ellie. *"Fly?"*

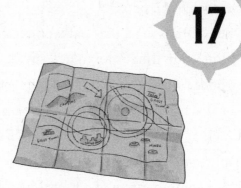

# 8 DAYS AGO

### BLIPSTREAM DIRECT MESSENGER

**Addie Earhart:** I made a list for you.

**JoJo12:** A list of what?

**Addie Earhart:** All the things you can do for a job without going to college. IT'S A VERY LONG LIST!

**JoJo12:** OK...

**Addie Earhart:** Elevator installer.

**JoJo12:** I'm not really all that interested in elevators.

**Addie Earhart:** Really? They actually make a lot of money. How about nuclear power reactor operator? How cool does that sound?

**JoJo12:** Sounds dangerous.

**Addie Earhart:** Boilermaker.

**JoJo12:** I don't even know what that is.

**Addie Earhart:** Me neither. How about an electrician?

**JoJo12:** What if I electrocute myself?

**Addie Earhart:** Artist. You do like to draw, right?

**JoJo12:** Yeah, but I don't know if I'm very good at it. Plus my art teacher always says she's a "starving artist," and I don't like being hungry all the time.

**Addie Earhart:** You like travel books. You could become a professional traveler who writes those books. I don't think writers have to go to college. They just have to be good at writing.

**JoJo12:** I don't think I am.

**Addie Earhart:** Well, what else are you interested in?

**JoJo12:** I like reading about explorers.

**Addie Earhart:** I'm not sure there's a job for that, but I've given you TONS of good options. A PLETHORA of choices. ENDLESS possibilities.

**JoJo12:** I think you might make a good VOCABULARY teacher.

**Addie Earhart:** No, I belong in the sky.

# NOW

Ellie smiles. "Oh yeah! I should've introduced you. That there was one of the very first woman pilots!" Ellie gets all serious. "*Ever.* You ought to go watch her take off."

I hop off my stool. "Will you please watch my phone?" I quickly ask Ellie, and she nods. Then I push my way outside into the shocking heat and run down the steps and across the dirt parking lot to the landing strip, where Joanie's walking toward a small plane, little puffs of dust floating behind her every footstep.

I stop before the landing strip, but Joanie must

have heard me because she turns around. "What's up, Bertha?"

I swear I want to burst out laughing every time I hear that name. *Marty*.

"I just..." I say, shifting from foot to foot. "Are you Joanie Cash?"

"The one and only."

"One of the first woman pilots?"

"Well, *commercial* pilots." She smiles. "There were great woman pilots before me."

"I wanted to watch you take off. I didn't know you flew here."

"You got an interest in flying?" she asks.

"Yeah, but I've never been in a plane before."

Her mouth drops open. "My dear, you must remedy that as soon as possible."

If only it were that easy. "My friend is a big fan of yours," I say. "She wants to be a pilot when she grows up."

"Uh-huh. And what do you want to be?"

I dig my sneaker into the packed dirt. "Do you really think I could be an artist?"

"You *are* an artist."

"But what if I don't have any money? Like, to go to college and stuff?"

Joanie takes a few steps so she's right in my face. "Listen here, Bertha," she says all seriously. "I was poor trailer trash from some nowhere little desert town. Everyone told me I could never be a pilot. They laughed at me. 'Girls aren't pilots,' they said." She snorts. "What a boys' club flying was." She frowns. "Well, still is."

"But you showed them."

"And you'll show them, too. Because there are things in this world more valuable than money."

"Like what?" I ask.

Joanie smiles. "Like having heart."

"But everyone has a heart," I say. "Or they'd be dead."

She laughs. "We all have *a* heart but we don't all *have heart*. I can tell you do." She sticks out her hand. "You take care of yourself."

Staring at Joanie's hand, I consider asking her to fly over the area to look for Addie. I want to so badly I could cry. But then everyone would know we lied about our reasons for being here. Would

Joanie believe me about Addie? Would they call the police? Can I risk it when I'm *this* close? After I've come all this way? Why does this have to be so stinking hard?

I slowly place my hand in Joanie's. "You too," I whisper.

She holds my hand a moment. "Are you okay, Bertha? You don't look so well."

"Oh, I'm okay. I haven't eaten much. I'm fine. Going to go in and finish my breakfast."

Joanie squeezes my hand. I watch as she gets in her plane, starts it up, and drives it to the far end of the landing strip. She waves at me from the cockpit, and I wave back. Then the plane is speeding down the strip, and despite the heat and the dull pain throbbing in my head, I can't stop myself from running after it, from feeling the hot wind in my face. I pretend I'm taking off, too.

## 18

"WHAT ARE YOU DOING OUT HERE?" I HEAR MARTY CRY. She's sprinting toward me.

"I was watching someone take off." I cover my mouth and cough the dust out of my lungs.

"I thought you were trying to ditch me again." She breathes heavily.

"I'm sorry."

She shields her eyes, watching the plane soar away from us. "Who's that?"

"That was the woman at the counter."

Marty's eyes flash. "She has a *plane*? Did you ask her to look for Addie?"

I take a step back. "No. How could I explain that?"

Marty throws her hands up. "Cuss, Jolene! She could've helped us."

"It wasn't worth the risk."

"And what kind of risk do you think we're taking going out there today? It would have been worth a shot!"

I can tell she's super mad at me, maybe for good reason. I wish she could understand. "I didn't know if we could trust her."

"Could you be any more paranoid, Jolene? What's the worst that could happen?"

"She could call the police."

"So what?"

"So they would take us both home, and Addie would die!"

"No, maybe getting our parents involved would be the best thing."

"They can't be involved. The police can't come to my house!"

Marty stares at me. "Why?" She grabs my arm. "I deserve to know the truth, Jolene."

Suddenly, the door of the café opens, and Ellie steps out. "Aren't you girls going to come finish your food? It's getting cold."

I jerk my arm out of Marty's grip and stomp back to the café, where Marty and I sit quietly, finishing our breakfast. When Ellie brings out the bill, Marty slaps some money down.

"I'll pay you back," I mumble, though I'm not completely sure how.

"Don't worry about it," she says flatly. After Ellie brings Marty back her change, Marty says, "Let's get this over with."

I check the phone's battery. It's only managed to charge to 21 percent, but it will have to do. It's already late morning, getting hotter by the minute, and we need to reach Addie before the hottest time of day. I check the BlipStream messages one last time before turning on battery-saver mode. I won't use it again for any reason other than to check the map.

"So what do you two have planned for the rest of the day?" Ellie asks.

"Not much," Marty says, dumping both of our

ice waters into her empty salsa jar. "Just hiding out from the heat."

"That sounds about right," says Ellie. "Today is going to be bad."

I gaze out the window. It even *looks* hot out there. The air is all wavy and shimmery, like it's on fire or something.

Marty and I step down from our stools. Slipping her backpack over her shoulders, Marty asks, "Why are there ties all over the ceiling?"

Ellie laughs and pulls a cartoonishly large pair of scissors from under the counter. "If a stodgy man comes in here wearing a tie, we cut it right off. This ain't no swanky place."

Marty smiles and says, "Thanks for breakfast."

We step out into the morning heat. It's hard to believe it can get much hotter, but of course I don't say that as I put my sunglasses on. I'm pretty sure Marty is still mad at me for not asking Joanie to fly over the area and check for Addie. And for not telling her whatever she thinks I'm hiding.

Marty stops at an old picnic table and says,

"Give me your water." I don't want to frustrate her even more, so I hand over my jug without question. "Now give me your pencil." I do as she orders.

She scrapes a gray horizontal line across the middle of the plastic jug. "This," she says, pointing. "This is where we turn around. Got that?"

"But when we find Addie, we can call for rescue."

"*We'll* still have to get back, Jolene." She tilts her head. "Unless you want to be rescued, too. Which means the authorities will be involved, and then your mom will have to get involved." She pushes the jug toward me. "I know you don't want that."

I want to argue, but she's right. I can't risk a rescue call for myself. Just for Addie. Marty continues, "I'm drawing the line, Jolene. Literally."

I nod. "If it reaches the halfway mark, we'll turn back."

"And I'll know if you're not drinking as much as you should. I'm not going to let you kill yourself."

Marty and I walk through the metal gate and back down the dirt road to a four-way stop. I point in the direction of the mud canyon. "This is where we have to go," I say.

Marty waves a hand. "Lead the way, then."

"We'll probably be on this dirt road for a mile or so. The mud canyon should be at the end of it.

"What's a mud canyon?" Marty asks, staring straight ahead, not looking at me.

"It's a canyon made of mud."

"How do we get around it?"

"We have to go through it."

Marty breathes loudly. "How are we supposed to get through a canyon made of mud, Jolene?"

"It's all dried up. And I've seen Addie do it. She walked through the whole thing once on her show."

We don't speak again for a long time, the only sound our shoes crunching over the hard-packed dirt of the road. We come to a sun-faded stop sign. I look left and right, but there's only endless desert in both directions.

"Which way?" Marty asks in that same flat tone.

"Straight," I say with all the confidence I can muster, but my stomach is cramping again. Like this stop sign is a warning. *Stop and turn back now!* But there's no way we can stop now after we've come all this way.

I glance at Marty, but she's expressionless. She's probably thinking she's just going to get out here with me and get back as quickly as possible, and then I'll finally stop all this nonsense, and she can get rid of me free of guilt. She doesn't believe that Addie is in trouble. Like everyone else.

But I know Addie is out here. I know it. And I suddenly can't stop myself from thinking about what we might find when we reach her.

What if my location is off and we go to the wrong spot?

What if Addie's dehydration is too much?

What if the crash was *really* bad?

What if we're too late?

## 19

BY THE TIME WE REACH THE END OF THE DIRT ROAD, WE'VE already drunk a lot of our water. "At this rate, we won't be able to go very far," Marty says.

"We'll make it," I assure her. "My water isn't even a quarter gone yet."

But my head is pounding, and sweat runs down every part of me. I touch one finger to my pink shoulder and press, leaving a white dot that quickly vanishes back to pink. I wish we had sunblock at home that I could have brought, but Mom says it's cheaper to wear long sleeves. Who wants to wear long sleeves when it's over a hundred degrees out?

We reach a sign that reads, in big red block

letters, DO NOT ENTER WHEN FLOODED. "This looks safe," Marty says.

I look up at the brilliant blue sky—not a cloud in sight. "There's no way it's going to rain today," I say. "And it hasn't rained in months." Then I take out my phone and map to check our location. I'm shocked to see the phone has somehow already dropped to 16 percent.

"What's wrong?" asks Marty.

"My phone battery is dropping," I say. Then I shrug. "It's okay. We still have enough."

Marty snatches the phone and looks at it, then hands it back. "It's an old phone, and it's hot," she says. "I hope it's going to last because I don't know how you think we're going to get help for Addie if it's dead by the time we reach her."

"Do you think I should turn it off?"

"Maybe, but then you'll need to turn it back on every time you want to check our location."

I stare at the phone, not sure what to do. I'm worried I won't be able to turn it back on if I turn it off. I'm worried it won't last. I'm worried it will overheat and die. I'm worried I'll reach the line on the water jug and Marty will make us turn back. I'm worried I'll have come this far and Addie will die anyway.

The car-crash feeling is so strong that I can feel it spreading into my fingertips. I decide to keep the phone on and slip it into my pocket. Then we walk into the most barren desert I've ever seen— no plants or cactuses anywhere. Just rivers of fine reddish sand and mounds of layered, brown, hard, cracked mud. The crunching of our shoes becomes muffled pats on the soft, pinkish-brown ground.

"It looks like Mars, huh?" I say.

Marty shrugs. "I wouldn't know. I've never been to Mars." She glances at me and her lip turns up a little at one corner. Then she stops. "Whoa. Look at that." She points ahead at a raised area with a wide slit at the center.

"I think that's where we enter the mud canyon," I tell her, pulling out my map to double-check. Taking deep breaths of burning air, I long for the shade of the canyon.

We move toward the giant walls of mud, but just as we reach the opening, an animal bursts out. My heart skips a beat, surprise gripping my whole body, freezing me in place. Marty lets out the highest-pitched screech I've ever heard. "Cuss!" she cries.

The donkey runs past us, making a loud screeching noise, and I'm finally able to move enough to look at Marty. Her hands cover her face, and she's peering through her fingers like a little kid watching a scary movie. We both burst out laughing.

"I totally forgot there are donkeys out here," I say through breathless laughter, which hurts my already aching head. "You look scared to death."

"I was!" she cries. "I thought it was a mountain lion or coyote or something." She finally lowers her hands. "The thing sounds like a T. rex. What the heck are they doing out here anyway?"

I try to remember what Addie said on her show. "I think miners brought them here a long time ago," I say. "And they've been here ever since."

We stand at the entrance of the canyon, laughing. "Do you think there are any more in there?" Marty asks.

I shrug. "They won't hurt us, you know."

"They might kick us," she says. "With their big donkey hooves."

"They're not going to kick us," I say, grabbing her arm and pulling her along. "Come on."

Once we're inside, Marty asks, "How long to get through this thing?"

"Not long. Maybe thirty minutes, max."

Marty kicks a giant block of mud, and pieces crumble off. "What if one of these big blobs of mud is in our way?"

"I guess we'll have to climb over."

Marty raises an eyebrow. "And what if a big blob of mud falls on our heads." She points up at a perilously perched ball of mud hanging from the rim.

I smirk. "We'll just hope it falls on you and not me."

"Actually it would be better if it hit your head." Marty rubs her knuckles over my hair. "You have the hardest head of anyone I've ever met in my life. Nothing is cracking that skull."

I laugh and push her hand away. "Look who's talking."

Small caves and strange tunnels to nowhere dot the canyon walls. I peek into one dark tunnel and see that it curves back into the canyon. Marty sticks her head in the other side and shouts, "Hello! Can you hear me?" even though she's only about twenty feet away.

The farther we go, the higher the walls of mud rise, until they're about fifty feet high, giving us much needed relief from the direct sun. I remove my hazy sunglasses. "This shade feels amazing," I say.

Marty pulls a large chunk off the wall. It breaks away easily and crumbles in her hands. "As long as these walls don't collapse and smother us," she says.

The walls do look crumbling and brittle enough to break apart and fall on top of us. Marty points out every chunk that has come loose and exploded on the canyon floor. "I guess this happens when it floods," she says.

I gaze at the looming walls, looking for something I recognize, but maybe the canyon has changed since I last saw it on Addie's video. Even though it doesn't help us, I like that this canyon grows and changes so drastically with every single storm. I like that it's never stuck being only one thing forever.

Then I spot an old gnarled ironwood tree growing up out of the path of floods—one of the only living things in all this crackled and crumbling gray. "I recognize that tree," I tell Marty, my heart racing with excitement, with knowing we're going the right way and will find Addie soon. "We're almost out of here."

Marty nods and walks ahead of me, but I don't follow her. She stops and turns around. "You coming?"

"I just...I want you to know I really appreciate you doing this with me. You didn't have to do this."

Marty's face softens. "You're welcome."

I dig my dirt-covered sneaker into a patch of cracked ground. "No one has ever gone out of their way like this for me."

"No one?"

"No."

"What about your mom?"

"Well, you know, she has to do stuff for me because she's my mom." I've said what I wanted to say, and now I want to move on. I walk around Marty.

"Don't you have any other family?" Marty asks, catching up to me. "Like cousins or something?"

"I have an aunt."

"Are you guys close?"

I shake my head. "No, not really. Well, this one time she watched me for a couple of days when my mom was in the hospital after we got in a car accident, so I guess she helped me once. But I don't know where she is now. Before my mom was able to come home, she dropped me off at the hospital and took off. I haven't seen her since."

Marty's mouth drops open. "You mean she just *dumped* you?"

I nod, trying to hold back the tears. There's no point in crying about it now. Aunt Mallory's not worth it. "Like a bag of trash," I whisper to the canyon wall.

Marty furrows her eyebrows. "You, Jolene, are *not* a bag of trash."

I blink, focusing on the winding path in front of me, hoping it opens back up soon.

"What happened after she dropped you at the hospital?"

"I asked to see my mom, but she wasn't awake— she'd broken her arm, ribs, and hip. She'd hit her head really hard, too. She was in bad shape, and they couldn't even ask her about where I should go. The nurses were so nice to me, though, you know? They got me food from the cafeteria and brought me a puzzle to play with. And then CPS showed up."

Marty gives me a sideward glance. "Child Protective Services?"

I nod. "Yeah. They called them. All that time they'd been acting so nice to me, they were waiting for CPS to show up and get me out of their hair."

Marty's quiet a moment. "Then what happened?"

I try to swallow, but my throat is so dry and tight that I can't. "We really shouldn't waste any more time talking about this," I say hoarsely. "We need to save our energy."

"Why don't you answer the question?" says Marty.

"There's not much more to say. I didn't have

anywhere else to go, so I stayed with this family I'd never met. Emergency foster care."

"I'm sorry."

I shrug off Marty's words. "It's fine. They were nice to me. I only had to be there a few weeks until Mom got out of the hospital."

"Still," says Marty. "That must have been really hard. And scary."

I'm finally able to swallow. "Anyway, it just means a lot to me that you're willing to do this. I know you might get into trouble for it, too."

She looks at me and smiles, but only with her mouth. Her eyes look sad. "Sometimes helping a friend means we have to make some kind of sacrifice, right?"

I blink away the last tears, putting my sunglasses on to hide them. "Right."

"So..." Marty says. "How's your mom now? Sounds like she got hurt pretty badly."

"She's okay, I guess. She lost her job because it was too hard for her to work anymore. But she's okay."

Marty stops. The canyon walls have gotten a lot smaller, and sunlight beats down on us now. "Are you sure about that?" Marty asks.

I turn and face her. "Why wouldn't I be sure?"

"Because you sound unsure."

"My mom is fine. I mean, she still has pain. She struggles to do much anymore."

"Is that hard on you guys?"

I shrug. "It's fine. She gets disability money. We're fine."

Marty opens her mouth, but I run off, the thin soles of my worn sneakers slapping the dirt, pebbles stabbing my sore feet. "I see the opening! We're almost there," I call back, hoping she'll let the conversation drop.

She walks up beside me, and we scan the landscape—hills and small mountains all around dotted with palo verde trees and saguaro cactuses. I know we're not in the exact right spot yet, but my heart sinks a little when there's no sign of Addie anywhere.

"I'm glad we didn't have to drink as much water

in the canyon," I say, taking out my jug. The water is about a quarter gone. "Plenty of water left to find Addie." I open my map. "We're close."

"How close?" asks Marty.

Looking at the endless desert before us, at all the brown and green and pale pink, I hope for the smallest pop of bright red. There is none, but I tell Marty, "We'll find her soon."

## 20

# 5 DAYS AGO

## BLIPSTREAM DIRECT MESSENGER

**Addie Earhart:** Are you there, Jo?

**JoJo12:** I'm here. Not like I have anything better to do than sit here at the library.

**Addie Earhart:** Everything OK?

**JoJo12:** I'm just not feeling great. How are you?

**Addie Earhart:** I miss my dad. I miss flying the ultralight with him.

**JoJo12:** Why don't you have your mom come with you sometime?

**Addie Earhart:** OK, I feel like I should tell you something. My mom doesn't know I fly the ultralight.

**JoJo12:** Are you serious?? Then how do you do it without getting in trouble?

**Addie Earhart:** I only fly it when she's at work. That's why I livestream it—no chance of her seeing a video or anything. Phew! It feels good to get that off my chest. So what's going on with you? Why don't you feel well?

**JoJo12:** I remember when I was little, and I would get excited about stuff. Like Christmas or my birthday coming up or maybe going to a movie with my mom. I miss that. I never feel like I have anything to get excited about anymore.

**Addie Earhart:** You can get excited about our trip, remember?

**JoJo12:** That's never going to happen. Nothing ever changes or gets better. Everything is always the same.

# NOW

My head is hammering. I'm probably not drinking enough water, but I can't risk it getting close to the middle line and Marty making us go back before we find Addie.

Marty wipes the sweat pouring down her face. "How hot do you think it is?"

I shrug. "It's not that bad. Ninety maybe."

Marty laughs. "In your dreams. It's a hundred at least and getting hotter."

I know she's right. I feel every one of those one hundred degrees. My body aches, and my nausea has been getting worse with every degree the temperature rises.

The trail we're following winds around a small mountain. It's not terribly steep, but we're breathing hard and sweating, barely able to speak from the exertion. I look down. Along the edge of the path, the cliffside plummets about fifty feet to the desert floor. What if I slip? Could I grab a bush or something? I start to feel dizzy.

"Don't look down," Marty orders, and I quickly move my eyes to the trail in front of me.

On the other side of the mountain, I spot the wash, easy to see because it's the only place in all this brown where towering cottonwoods grow because of the extra water during storms. "There!" I point. "That's where we need to go."

I shield my eyes, hoping Marty doesn't notice how much my hand is shaking, and scan the area for any signs of Addie. I can't see the middle of the wash because of all the trees. Were there green trees when Addie was falling from the sky? It was so hard to tell what was happening, but I don't remember seeing so much green. It was more like a lot of brown with just a touch of green mixed in. A whole lot of brown.

"Moment of truth," Marty says. "If she's not down there, we're leaving, Jolene." She stares at me, apparently waiting for me to agree.

"I know," I say. "But she's down there."

Marty nods slowly. "If you say so."

Instead of snapping back at her that I *do* say so, I hurry down the mountain trail as fast as my unsteady legs can carry me, cut across the open desert, and run into the middle of the wash, my sneakers digging into the deep, loose sand, the trees providing some relief from the beating sun. My shoes fill with sand as I rush toward Addie's location.

My heart pounds with anticipation and hope. And sickness. And dread.

"Wait up, Jolene," Marty cries, but I don't wait. The waiting is killing me. I need to know that Addie is here. That she's alive. That I didn't come all this way for no reason. I finally round a corner and brace myself.

But there's nothing but more sandy wash.

No red ultralight.

No Addie.

I run along the wash into a shallow ravine at a fork.

Nothing.

I run back past Marty and take the other path at the fork.

"Jolene, wait!" Marty cries again.

There's nothing.

Having lost the strength to run anymore, I weakly jog along the wash, stumbling over the loose sand, pulling my hazy sunglasses off and looking in every direction. "Addie!" I scream. "Addie, where are you?" But there's nothing. I remember the car accident. Even days later, there were traces of it—glass and other debris that got missed, scuff marks in the street and sidewalk. There are no traces of any accident here.

"Addie!" I scream again with all the energy I have left. Combined with the pain shooting through my body and the overwhelming heat, the car-crash feeling is the worst it's ever been. There's not a box big enough to hold it this time.

I feel Marty's hand on my shoulder. "I'm sorry," she says, but I shrug her hand off. "Jolene." Marty's voice is soft and kinder than I deserve. "She's not here. You know we have to go back."

## 21

I DROP MY SUNGLASSES AND PULL THE JUG OUT OF MY backpack. The water is nearly at the midway line.

Marty steps in front of me. "You did all you could," she says. "You did your best."

I shake my head and drop the water on the sand next to my sunglasses. "And of course it wasn't good enough. It could never be good enough."

"That is *not* true," Marty says. "This was simply not possible."

"People do the impossible all the time," I say, my eyes filling. I don't even care if she thinks I'm a crybaby. What does it matter anymore? "But not me."

"You can do a lot, Jolene. But you never knew

for sure where Addie crashed. Or even *if* she crashed. Maybe you didn't see what you think you saw. I wouldn't be surprised if Addie's at home with her mom right now, and you keep putting yourself through this for no good reason."

"No good reason," I whisper.

Marty gently grabs my arm. "Now let's go."

I dig my feet into the sand and jerk my arm away. "I'm not leaving," I say through clenched teeth. "I'm not leaving until I find Addie."

Marty throws her hands up. "So what? You're just going to stay out here looking for her until you *die*? Which, by the way, will only take a few more hours. How is that going to help anyone?"

"Why not? No one would care."

Marty gapes at me. "You don't think *I* would care? You don't think your mom would care?"

Then all those stacked little boxes that have cluttered up my insides finally topple over and burst open. "No, I don't!" I shout, letting out all the tears I've ever held in.

Marty stares at me. "You're wrong."

"You don't know anything about me. We just

met." I wipe my sandy, stinging cheeks. "The only reason you're here is because you'd feel guilty if I died."

Marty winces. "Wrong again, Jolene. And the only reason I don't know more about you is because you won't tell me anything."

Marty's right. I haven't told her about the pills and the empty fridge and the kids at school and the car-crash feeling. I haven't told her about Benjamin being taken away and how I miss him so much that sometimes I can't stop crying in the middle of the night. I haven't told her about how someone left a note on my desk on the last day of the school year. How I'd thought it was a goodbye letter or maybe something that might say *Have a nice summer!* or—and this was a long shot—an invitation to an end-of-the-school-year party.

No, it was a hand-drawn picture of me. And in the picture, my teeth looked like a vampire's. My clothes looked like torn rags. And in big letters across the top: *Bye, Snaggletooth.*

So Marty will never understand why I needed to find Addie so badly, why this was so important to me. Because Addie was the first person in a long time to truly be my friend. She never cared about what I might have looked like or what kind of clothes I wore or how much money I had. And she listened to me. *Really* listened. I couldn't bear to lose that again.

And also, maybe if I saved Addie, they would all see that I'm more than they think. Maybe the kids at school would see that I'm more than I look. And maybe Mom would see that I'm enough to get better for. Maybe I could see those things, too.

I look at Marty. "Maybe if I found Addie, then everyone would think that what you said in the car is true—that I can do things."

"The only person who needs to believe that is *you*."

"How can I ever believe it? I can't do anything. I can't even find Addie. This should've been easy, but now she'll die because of me."

"No," Marty says, grasping my shoulders. "There's no one out here, Jolene. You can see now for yourself. No one is going to die. And even if Addie had been out here, it still wouldn't have been your fault. It's not your responsibility to save anyone from their own choices." She stares a hole right into my heart. "Not even your mom."

Her words hit me hard, and I don't care anymore if she knows about Mom. I hurt too much to care about anything else right now. "But their choices hurt me so bad."

Marty hugs me to her and squeezes. The heat of her body is overwhelming, but I don't pull away. "I know," she says softly. "I know. I really do."

But how could she? Marty is everything I'm not. Has everything I don't.

We stand there in the middle of the scorching desert together, my crying the only sound for miles around. Finally, Marty pulls away from me. "Jolene." She wipes my sunburned cheek. "It's time to go." She hands me the water and sunglasses. I put them in my backpack and follow her quietly back, shuffling my feet through the deep sand, leaving a trail that will probably get washed away before anyone ever sees it. Like I was never even there.

And then suddenly, there *is* another sound, something floating to us through the hot, thick air. I stop and listen, unmoving, trying not to breathe.

"What?" Marty asks, but I shush her. The sound is so faint. I worry it will fade away.

But there it is again—a gentle ting over and over again. Like metal on metal. There's nothing out here that could make that sound, especially at this time of day—no construction, no cars, no campers. Nothing except maybe . . .

I race in the direction of the sound.

"Jolene!" Marty cries, but I don't stop. I don't know how long the sound will last, and it's so faint that I'm afraid I'll lose it.

It gets slightly louder, and I change course, vaguely aware of Marty running behind me.

*Don't let the sound stop* is all I can think.

I hear it again, and quickly turn toward a hill above the wash.

*Please don't stop.*

I claw my way up the rocky hill, the blazing hot dirt searing my raw hands, cactuses tearing my legs, thorny trees and bushes snagging my torn and dirty clothes.

"Jolene!" Marty cries again.

I can't stop. Right now, in this moment, I am

Wanda Rutkiewicz, climbing K2. I am Lucy Walker, nearing the top of the Matterhorn. I am Junko Tabei, summiting Mount Everest. They are all with me, pushing me, giving me their strength.

I reach the top of the hill, sweat drenching my tank top, my arms and legs bleeding, my hands burning like fire.

I look down the other side.

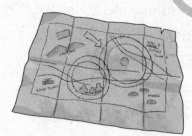

## 22

# 3 DAYS AGO

## BLIPSTREAM DIRECT MESSENGER

**JoJo12:** Why do you do the show? I mean, I know why you fly the ultralight, but why do you livestream it when there's a chance your mom might find out?

**Addie Earhart:** I guess it makes me feel like someone might be flying with me. Like my dad is still with me. Sometimes I wake up in the morning, and I forget he's dead. Can you believe that? I've even picked up the phone to call him a couple of times. And the other day, I was working on something, and I called out for him to help me. I actually called out, "Dad!" You should've seen the look on my mom's face.

Then I ran out of the room because I didn't know what to say to her.

**JoJo12:** Sometimes I forget my mom is sick. Sometimes I think, *I need to talk to Mom about this.* And then I remember she won't care.

**Addie Earhart:** Next time you need to talk to someone, you can talk to me.

**JoJo12:** And next time you need help with something, you can call for me.


# NOW


I see it.

The red ultralight is at the bottom of the hill, smashed against a big boulder, the wing bent, debris scattered around it.

Addie still strapped in the driver's seat.

I scan the hill for the best route down, but there's no clear path. I can hear Marty scramble up behind me. "What do you see?" she calls.

"She's there! I see her."

Marty makes it to the top, with her tank top,

arms, and legs all torn up. She stands next to me, panting, bleeding, sweat running down her face. Her mouth drops open. "Holy…cuss," she whispers.

"We have to get down," I say.

"Right." Marty nods her head furiously. "Quickly." We cut a trail as well as we can between bushes and cactuses, our legs more and more bloodied with every step. Where the hill is too steep, we slide on our butts, and the blazing hot ground burns the backs of our thighs.

We reach the bottom and run to Addie. She hit the boulder head-on, crushing the front of the ultralight and pinning her legs against the rock. Addie's face and arms are burned to blistering. Her helmet lies on the ground, the cell phone she uses to record no longer attached.

She's holding her metal canteen with the cap hanging off. Her eyes remain closed as she lifts the canteen weakly and strikes it against the ultralight frame. I reach out and take the canteen from her, then hold her hand in mine. Addie's eyes flutter open. "Who—" she begins, but Marty interrupts.

"We need to call now," she says. "We don't have a second of battery life to spare."

She's right. I whip out my phone, and Marty grabs it and dials 911. I hold Addie's hand again.

"I heard you," Addie says, her voice hoarse, barely above a whisper, like her throat is filled with sand. I have to lean in to understand her. "I heard you shouting."

"Good," I say, squeezing her hand. "That's good."

"Yes, hello," Marty says, her voice filled with panic. "We need help. We're here with—" Marty looks at Addie. "What's your name?" she demands.

"Adelaide," Addie says.

"Your full name?" Marty says impatiently.

"Oh, it's Adelaide Chapman."

"Yes, I'm here with Adelaide Chapman. She's probably been reported missing. We're here out in…Hello?" Marty pulls the phone away from her ear and stares at it, punching repeatedly at the power button. "Oh, cuss!" she shouts. "Curse and swear and all the bad words!"

I suck in a deep breath and fight the dizziness. "I take it the phone is dead."

Marty screams at the sky. "I can't believe this cussing luck!"

I scan the area around the ultralight. "Where's your phone?" I ask Addie. "What happened to it?"

Addie weakly lifts her arm and points. "There."

Marty stomps over and picks up the phone. "It's smashed," she says, hitting the power button. "Dead." She slips the phone into her backpack, then wipes her forehead and breathes in. "We can't call for help anymore."

"I'm so thirsty," Addie says, barely above a rasp, like her voice is as sunburned as her skin. "My water is gone."

I quickly open my pack and hold the water jug to her dry, cracked lips. Addie grips the container, and I'm glad to see that her hands are okay, unlike her legs. She coughs on the first sip and then gulps greedily, water pouring down her mouth, which I can't bear to see wasted. I adjust the jug so it's not pouring so quickly into her mouth. I worry about the amount of water she's drinking, but I also know she must desperately need it. If she hadn't had her canteen, she'd probably be dead by now.

Addie blinks her eyes open. "Do you think I'm paralyzed?" she asks. "I can barely feel my legs anymore."

I force myself to look down, but I can't see all of her legs. "Could you feel them after the crash?" I ask.

"Yes," she says. "It was the worst pain I ever felt in my life. Then after a while they went numb."

"You're not paralyzed," Marty says. "Your legs might be broken, but your spine is probably fine."

"You'll be okay," I assure her, but I'm not actually sure. We can't call for help, and we don't have nearly enough water for the three of us to get back. And how would Addie get back? We'd probably have to carry her out of here. That's impossible.

"I guess I can still fly, even if I am paralyzed," Addie croaks out, closing her eyes again. "You don't need legs to fly."

I tell her, "No, you just need wings."

Addie opens her eyes and squints at me in the bright sunlight. "Who *are* you?"

I smile. "I'm Jolene. It's nice to finally meet you."

## 23

"SO, NEW PLAN," MARTY SAYS. "WE NEED A NEW PLAN. A brand-new plan. Some kind of plan."

"What happened?" I ask Addie. "One minute everything seemed fine, and then you were falling from the sky."

She takes a deep breath. "When the propeller cut out, I couldn't find a safe place to land. I hit this boulder so hard it made my phone fly out of my helmet, and I couldn't reach it. It's kind of good I'm next to the boulder, though, because it blocked the sun for half the day."

Marty shakes her head. "I wouldn't exactly call

hitting that boulder a good thing. We have to move. You're already blistering."

"There's a mine," Addie tells us. "We can go inside it. We just have to get there."

"How far?" I ask.

"I don't know," says Addie. "Not far."

Marty and I look at each other. However far "not far" is will still feel very far in this heat. We need to save as much water as we can. And we'll have to figure out a way to carry Addie.

"I don't know how we're going to do this with what water we have left." Marty wrings her hands. "How are we supposed to get back?" She kicks the dirt. "Stupid cussing phones. Stupid cussing toilets."

It occurs to me that Marty wouldn't even be here if she hadn't dropped her phone in the toilet. She's probably thinking it was the biggest mistake of her life right about now.

Addie stares at Marty. "Toilets?"

"Yeah," I say. "Marty dropped her phone in the toilet."

Addie says, "What kind of rescuers are you?"

Marty snorts. "Good enough to find your cracker pants self."

I look down at Addie's legs pinned against the big rock. "I'm sorry," I say. "We need to pull you away from the boulder."

"I know." Addie looks up at me with scared eyes, then closes them and slowly nods. "The ultralight doesn't weigh much. It should be easy to pull away."

Marty walks around the ultralight, studying the wheels and the area around them. She seems nervous. We don't know what we're going to find when we pull the ultralight away—what Addie's legs might look like. If we're even able to move her at all.

Marty motions for me to join her behind the ultralight, and we each grip one bar. "On the count of three," Marty says. "One, two, three."

We both pull the ultralight back, and Addie lets out a hoarse scream. Her jeans and boots are dark red with blood. Memories of the car accident flood my mind, making my head spin. Before I get too dizzy, I look away and bend down in front of Addie. Her raspy screams have turned to whispered sobs.

"Here." I grab her hands. "Squeeze my hands as tightly as you need to. You won't hurt me."

Addie puts her flaccid hands in mine, but she doesn't have the strength to grip. She closes her eyes and buries her head in my shoulder. "It hurts," she whispers.

"That's good," I tell her. "It's good that you can feel them."

"They don't look that bad," Marty says. "Maybe broken, but they're really not that bad."

Addie cries into my shoulder. When she lifts her head, I notice she has no tears at all despite how hard she's been crying, like her body doesn't have a drop of water left to spare. And her cheeks are bubbling with little fluid-filled blisters.

I look up at Marty. "We've got to get her out of the sun right away. Us too."

"If the mine isn't too far," says Marty, "I think maybe I can carry you piggyback, letting your legs hang down."

Marty leans down, and Addie wraps her bright red arms around her neck. But when Marty stands back up, Addie's arms slip off. "I'm sorry," she says. "I don't think I can hold on."

I study the ultralight. "Maybe we can push her," I say. "Push her in the ultralight. I mean, it does have wheels. And Addie was right. It's not heavy."

"Yeah, but one wheel is smashed," says Marty.

"We pulled her away from the boulder," I say. "It still rolls."

"I think that could work," says Addie. "It's mostly wash between here and the mine. There shouldn't be anything in our way."

Marty and I pull the ultralight farther back from the boulder, then push hard in the direction Addie guides us. I know immediately this is going to take way too much energy, and way too much water.

I probably sweat out more than I've drunk as we push Addie over the hard dirt. I hadn't thought it was possible for the pounding in my head to get worse, but it does, and I know that pushing Addie out of here in the direct sun would be absolutely impossible. I'm already feeling like I'm at my end when we reach the wash, and it somehow gets even harder to push. Marty and I grunt and pant, trying to get through the loose sand. We have to stop several times to take sips of water, doing our best to conserve as much as possible. And a couple of times, I have to grip my legs and bend down when my vision starts going black. I can't pass out and make Marty deal with this alone.

By the time we make it to the mine, we don't have nearly enough water to get back. Marty's jar is empty, and my water is well below the halfway line. But even if we had more water, I know we couldn't push Addie back in this sun. No amount of water would keep us from getting sunstroke and badly burned. I doubt I could even stay conscious with so much exertion.

We push the ultralight as close as we can to the mine's opening—a rounded wooden wall cut into the stone face of a mountain. It looks like it used to have a door. Barbed wire guards the opening, and a sign warns DANGER! STAY OUT! STAY ALIVE!

Marty says, "Well, today we have to stay in to stay alive."

"Do you think we can die if we go in there?" I ask.

"No," says Addie. "I've gone in there before."

Marty shakes her head and rolls her eyes. "Of course you have, daredevil. But that's not reassuring."

"We should stay as close to the opening as possible," I say. "It's too dark in there anyway to go very far. But how are we going to get Addie through the barbed wire?" This whole ordeal feels like obstacle after obstacle. I know this is what explorers face, but reading about it sure is different from living it.

"There's a shovel inside," says Addie. "Maybe you can do something with that. There's also an old mining cart. Maybe you can build some kind of ramp over the barbed wire and push me in the cart. Or you can build some kind of support to hold the fence up and then you can push me under it."

Marty walks along the barbed-wire fence until she reaches the weather-beaten wooden post that's holding it up. She kicks it until it falls over. "Or I can do that," she says, pulling the post to one side, the barbed wire going with it. "Good thing everything around here is old as heck."

Marty and I grip hands underneath Addie, and she wraps her arms around our necks. "We only have to carry you a few feet," I tell her, though I'm worried about my ability to carry her at all with the way I feel—shaky, queasy, aching, near fainting. I can't wait to get out of the sun.

I look at Marty and we lift. Addie's surprisingly light, but she cries out in pain as we move her up and over the front of the ultralight. The way we have to hold her in a seated position over our arms like this is awkward and makes it difficult for both me and Marty to walk, especially as we maneuver through the narrow doorway. My arms shake with fatigue, and as strong as Marty is, I can see she's worn out and struggling to hold Addie.

"Almost there," Marty grunts, and we set her down as gently as we can against the mine wall, close to the doorway but out of the direct sunlight, where she sobs softly to herself.

"Are you okay?" I ask, sitting down next to her. I know there's no way we can carry her like that all the way back to the Flipside Café. My arms were already burning and about to give out by the time we set her down. And even if Marty and I somehow could carry her that far, Addie couldn't stand the pain for that long.

"It hurts so bad," Addie says.

I pat her shoulder. "Don't worry. We're going to get out of here and get help."

"How are we going to do that?" asks Marty. "We don't have enough water."

Addie wipes her nose. "Unless someone else shows up, we'll have to wait until dark. I want to call my mom." Addie cries harder. "She's going to be so mad at me."

I continue patting her shoulder. "I don't think she'll be mad. She'll probably just be happy you're home." That makes me wonder how Mom will feel when I get home. Will she be mad, or will she be happy I'm back? Does she even realize I'm gone yet? Probably, but only because of the phone.

"I'll never get to fly again," Addie wails.

But Marty is still focused on our plan. "All we have is Jolene's map, which will be hard to read in the dark. How do we find our way back without a phone?"

Addie sniffles. "And the rattlesnakes will be out."

I know that all too well. "We can't just sit here and wait for someone until we dehydrate," I say. "We didn't see a single other person out here today."

"No one's out here during the summer," says Addie.

Marty grunts. "Except you apparently."

"We have to get out of here," I say. "No matter what that takes. Staying here is not an option." And Addie badly needs to get to a hospital. Even if her legs aren't broken, her skin needs care. I've never seen such a bad sunburn before.

"How did you get here?" asks Addie, and I pull out the map to show her our path. She shakes her head. "We can't go back that way. There's a better route."

"But we don't know this better route," says Marty, running her hands through her blond and blue hair. She sits down and pulls her knees up to her face and lets her head fall onto them.

"Can I write on this?" Addie asks, and I pull out a pencil. With her shaking, sunburned hand, she traces an unsteady line from the mine, through the desert on the other side from where we came from, back to the Flipside Café. "There are no mountains going this way," she explains.

"But that's thick desert," I say. "I can see it all online. There's no trail."

"It's desert for a little bit, but they cut a new trail about a year ago not far from here," Addie says. "The maps you've been looking at are probably old."

"You sure about this?" asks Marty.

Addie nods. "I know this area better than anyone. This will be an easier way back."

Addie also writes down her mom's name, phone number, and address, in case she loses consciousness or something. I can't stand the thought of trying to get help again without having this information. I work at darkening the lines on my map so it will be easier to read at night.

Addie's stomach growls loudly, and Marty's head shoots up. "Was that you?" she asks. "I thought it was a mountain lion for a second." Her eyes dart around the mine. "Wait, there aren't any around here, are there?"

"Sure there are," Addie says. "And I'm starving. I haven't eaten since yesterday morning."

"Of course," I say, pulling my backpack off. "We have food."

Marty says, "Sorry, but Jolene has a can of sardines, and I have some hard-boiled eggs, prunes, and Ensure."

Addie says, "I don't care. I'd eat anything right now."

But when Addie takes a sip of Ensure, she gags it back up. She tries a prune, but the same thing happens. She can't keep anything down and starts crying again.

Marty shakes her head slightly and gives me a meaningful look, like she's trying to communicate how serious this is. I know how serious this is.

"That's okay," I tell Addie. "You don't need to eat right now. Just keep sipping a little water." But Marty and I are going to need the energy, so we eat quietly while Addie sporadically moans and grunts in pain. I feel kind of bad eating in front of her, but we have to keep our strength up for whatever it is we're going to have to do to get out of here.

When we're done, I ask Marty, "Think of a new plan yet?"

"Not yet," she says, leaning back against the wall and looking up at the stone ceiling. She sniffs and wipes her eyes. She seems completely worn out. Worried. Defeated.

As hot as it is in the mine, the shade and food have helped my dizziness, so I go and push on the old mining cart. The wheels screech and barely turn. "Well, that won't work." I sigh and resist the urge to kick the metal cart—I don't need to break my foot right now.

I stare at the ultralight through the doorway. We can't possibly push Addie in it all the way—it's too bulky and the front wheel is wrecked. Just pushing her to the mine was exhausting. But…

"Maybe we can use the ultralight parts to build something," I say. I remember how they carried Mom away after the car accident. "We can tear the fabric off the ultralight wing," I say. "Maybe we can make a stretcher. There's a whole lot of fabric on that ultralight. And maybe we could detach the back wheels somehow?" I ask Addie.

She grimaces. "I guess, maybe you could. There's a small tool kit under the driver's seat."

"Why didn't you say that before?" asks Marty.

"I didn't know it was important," says Addie. "And I'm saying it now."

"All information is important," says Marty. "Especially stuff we can use."

"I also have a snake skin and a stuffed animal under the back seat," Addie says. "Is that something you can use?"

Marty gapes at her. "No."

"Well, you said all information is important," says Addie.

"We'll still have to carry her," I say, bringing the conversation back. "But with a stretcher it shouldn't be as painful for her or awkward for us. And if we could somehow attach it to the wheels, it might not be very hard at all for us to pull her like one of those roller suitcases."

"I don't know," says Marty, appearing on the verge of tears. She's never seemed so anxious. She usually seems so in control. "Three miles in the dark, carrying Addie on a stretcher. We don't even know if we'll be able to get the ultralight apart or if we'll be able to put something together that will hold her."

I don't know if we'll be able to do it either. But I do know that a lot of people have done a lot of things that seemed impossible to the rest of the world. And maybe to themselves. This feels impossible now, but you never know what's truly possible until you do it.

## 24

IT'S STILL FLAMING HOT OUTSIDE, BUT WE CAN'T BUILD our stretcher in the dark, so we have to get our materials now. We find a Swiss Army knife in the tool kit and use it to cut and tear the fabric off the wing. There's so much of it that Marty excitedly wraps it around her body and exclaims, "This might just work, Jolene."

Then we find the right wrench to unscrew the bolts from the bars that make up the wing, and Marty beats them with the shovel until they come apart. We end up with two bars that seem like a good length for our stretcher.

"This is painful," Addie calls from inside the mine.

"Your legs?" I ask.

"No. Watching you guys tear my ultralight apart."

"Then avert your eyes, Adelaide," Marty says. "Avert your eyes."

We work at removing the back two wheels, and end up with two wheels and several shorter bars we hope to use to make a wheel base for our stretcher. We carry our materials back into the mine, where Addie is staring at the ground, her injured legs outstretched, her cheeks blazing red even in the shadowed mine. "I guess I thought it would still be okay," she mutters. "I thought maybe it could still be fixed. But probably not anymore."

"Girl, we have far more important things to worry about right now," Marty says.

Exhausted, I sit down next to Addie. "I'm sorry," I tell her. "Your life meant a whole lot more to your dad than that ultralight did."

"I know. I'm just sad to see it go." She wipes her

blistered cheeks and winces. I'm happy to see she has actual tears now.

Marty and I lay the two bars next to each other like a pair of skis. We spread the wing fabric out and attach it to the bars with fabric strips, bolts, and the fabric repair glue we found in the tool kit. It's a mess, and I hope the fabric stays in place. Then we work on making a wheel base for a stretcher, which we attach in the same haphazard way.

We help Addie onto the stretcher, carefully avoiding touching her legs. She shrieks with every movement, but we have to make sure it works. We help her lie back, then Marty grabs one bar and I grab the other, lifting her up at an angle. My weak, overheated, tired muscles quiver with the effort. I don't know what I was expecting—maybe that Addie would sit on top like a regular stretcher. Instead, her weight pushes the fabric down and the bars come together, closing over her head.

"It's an Addie taco," I say. "Good thing you like tacos, huh?"

But she doesn't laugh. I can hear her crying,

and then she starts to slide down a little. "Ow, my legs!" We quickly set her back down before she can slide more.

"This . . . is challenging," Marty says, rubbing her hands over her face. I worry for a second that she's going to start crying, and then I won't be able to stop myself from crying, and then we'll all be crying.

"A regular stretcher has, like, straps that go across," I say, again remembering Mom after the accident. So we make fabric straps to secure Addie in place. All this work distracts me from worrying about what's going to happen, about whether Addie's right about the trail. About whether I'll be strong enough to pull her through the desert on this flimsy thing.

We test the stretcher with our new straps, Addie whimpering in pain. But at least she doesn't slide down as much. I don't see any way we can keep this from being painful for her. We ease her back down, but when we try to lift her up to sitting, she sniffles and says, "Please just leave me here."

For a moment, I think she's asking us to leave her here in the mine, which I could never do. Then I realize she doesn't want us to move her off the stretcher—every movement must hurt terribly. So Marty and I sit on either side of her.

"How long do you think before it gets dark?" I ask Marty.

She shrugs. "A few hours maybe."

A few hours of sitting here doing nothing. Just sitting here waiting to see if we can make it back. *If.* I can't bear to sit here and think about what might happen if we can't make it through the desert in the dark. Can't bear to sit here with Marty, whose face is completely filled with fear, and Addie, who keeps moaning and sniffling. "We need to play a game or something," I say. "You know, to keep Addie distracted from the pain. We can't do anything until it gets dark anyway."

"I don't think Addie's up for basketball right now," Marty says. "We should try to sleep." She runs her hands over her hair and fidgets with her earrings, like she's having trouble sitting still. "If that's even possible," she whispers, and I wonder what she's thinking, if she believes we can make it.

Addie sniffs. "I wish I were at home playing Life with my mom. She always lets me be the yellow car," she bawls, like it's the saddest thing anyone's ever said.

"That game sucks," says Marty, now picking at her blue nail polish. "I don't like games that are all chance, especially a game about *life*." Then she sighs and leans back on her hands. "Let's play two truths and a lie. Addie goes first."

"What's that?" asks Addie, rubbing her nose.

"You've never played?" asks Marty, her voice filled with disbelief.

"Is this a school game?" asks Addie. "Because I was homeschooled up until recently."

"No," says Marty. "You say three facts about yourself. Two are true and one's a lie, and we have to guess the lie."

"Okay," says Addie. Then she's quiet a little while except for her grunting. "I miss my mom." Her voice quivers. "I miss my dad. I want to go home." She starts crying again.

"I don't think Addie understands the rules of this game," says Marty, while I pat Addie's head, trying to comfort her. "I'll show her how it's done." Marty clears her throat. "The first fact is that I can't stand hard-boiled eggs and prunes. The second fact is that…I didn't really believe anyone was out here until the moment I saw the ultralight." She looks at me, and her eyes seem a little bit more glimmery in the faint light. "I'm sorry about that," she says softly.

"It's okay," I tell her. "You still came with me."

Marty looks away from me. "And the third fact is that I'm going to be a psychiatrist."

I remember Marty saying she was going to be a doctor in the car—a doctor who helps people with addictions. "Is a psychiatrist a doctor?" I ask.

"Yes," says Marty. "They deal with mental health."

"That one," says Addie, hiccupping. "The psychiatrist one is the lie."

"Why do you think that?" asks Marty.

"Because you're probably going to be a professional wrestler," says Addie.

Marty and I both laugh. "Actually, I really like prunes," Marty says, popping one into her mouth. "Delicious." She chews it for a second and swallows. "Okay, Jolene's turn."

I sit and think for a second. "Okay, the first fact is that I love chicken nuggets. The second fact is that if I could have anything in the whole wide world, it would be braces. And the third fact is that I kind of... sort of maybe think I want to be some kind of artist or writer when I grow up. Maybe both. Maybe, like, for a travel magazine or something like that."

Marty stares at me, and I know that she knows the truths. But Addie says, "The braces thing is the lie. Who cares about that?"

Spoken like someone who was homeschooled for most of her life. "That's wrong," I say. "Actually, I hate chicken nuggets."

Marty says, "You don't need braces to be an artist or a writer, Jolene. Why don't you try wishing a bit bigger?"

Somehow Marty always has a way of making me feel... ashamed. Not ashamed of myself exactly. She makes me feel ashamed of how small I see myself. Of how little I think of myself. She makes me doubt all the things I've always believed. But I don't tell her that. Instead, I say, "Time for a new game. Marty, truth or dare?"

"Dare."

I think a moment. "I dare you to hold your breath for twenty seconds."

"That's it?"

"Well, what do you want me to dare you to do? I dare you to go outside and bite a lizard's tail off with your bare teeth."

Addie grunts and shifts onto her side. "I'll need my camera if you're going to do that."

"Here, I'll show you how it's done," Marty says. "Addie, truth or dare?"

"Dare."

"Okay," says Marty. "I dare you to tell me what compelled you to come out here in the desert and fly the ultralight behind your mom's back. Why was this so important to you that you would risk your whole life for it?"

"Hey," I say. "That's not fair. You turned dare into a truth."

Marty smirks. "Yeah, I'm sly like that."

Addie's quiet awhile. Finally she says softly, "I didn't think I was risking my life." We wait. I also want to hear the rest, even though I don't necessarily approve of Marty's prying with the condition Addie's in. "My dad used to take me up in it. I always felt safe with him. And happy. After he died, I wasn't happy anymore. Flying the ultralight makes me feel like he's still with me."

"Why didn't you just tell your mom that?" Marty asks.

Addie coughs. "She never would've let me fly the ultralight alone. It always made her nervous when my dad and I flew. She was trying to sell it."

"How did you get away with it for so long?" asks Marty.

"Sorry," I say. "Marty's kind of nosy in case you haven't figured that out yet."

"That's okay," Addie says. "It feels good to tell someone this since I might die."

"You're not going to die," Marty says. "But tell us anyway."

"We pay to keep the ultralight in a lot near our house. I'd wait for Mom to leave for work, then I'd check in with my grandma—tell her I'm good, just gonna watch some shows and eat snacks and all that. If she ever called to check on me and I was out, I'd call her back and tell her I didn't hear the phone ringing for some reason."

Marty clucks her tongue. "That's a lot of lies."

"I'm not proud of it," says Addie.

"What about gas?" asks Marty. "Doesn't it take gas?"

"The lot has a pump. It doesn't take much gas." Addie yawns and grunts, starts talking more slowly. "I'm so tired."

I'm exhausted, too. My eyelids feel like weights are tugging on them. I lie down next to Addie, and Marty does the same. The ground is hard and uncomfortable. Staring up at the dark mine ceiling, I say softly, "Ynéz Mexía traveled all over South America, along the entire Amazon River, and she constantly slept outdoors."

"Who's Ynéz Mexía?" Marty asks, her voice thick and slow.

"She was an explorer who studied plants," I say, closing my eyes. "If we can get a couple of hours of sleep, maybe the trip back won't be so hard."

No one says anything else. Because we all know it's going to be hard no matter what.

## 25

## 2 DAYS AGO

### BLIPSTREAM DIRECT MESSENGER

**JoJo12:** I wish we could hang out in person. Do you have a best friend you can hang out with?

**Addie Earhart:** Not really. You?

**JoJo12:** No. I used to have a good friend. I guess he was like a best friend.

**Addie Earhart:** What happened?

**JoJo12:** He had to move. I don't know where he went, and then we moved and lost our old apartment phone, so he can't call me even if he wants to.

**Addie Earhart:** That stinks.

**JoJo12:** I miss having a best friend. If I ever had a best friend again, I would be very dependable. I would always be there when they needed me. Even if it was really hard. They could count on me. I'd be a really good friend.

**Addie Earhart:** That person would be lucky to have you for a friend.

# NOW

I have no idea what time it is when I open my eyes, but it's much darker in the mine, with the only sounds Marty's light snoring and Addie's rasping breaths. I feel for Addie and shake her arm gently, but she doesn't wake.

"Addie," I say. "Addie, it's getting dark." I shake her harder this time, but she still doesn't stir much, and her breathing sounds scary, like she's struggling for every breath. Her arm feels hotter than it should be, even in this heat.

"It's dark," Marty groans. "We need to get up."

"Something's wrong with Addie," I say, the

car-crash feeling building again. After the giant explosion before we found Addie, I thought maybe it was used up. But I guess it won't go away that easily. "She's not waking up."

Marty sits and crawls around me. "Addie," she says loudly.

Addie finally moans. She says something, but the words are a whispered jumble we can't understand.

"I think she has a fever," says Marty. "We've got to get out of here. She for sure has severe heat-stroke, and she might even have an infection. She could become septic."

"What does that mean?" I ask.

"She's probably getting an infection in one of her legs, and if we don't get her help soon, it can spread in her blood. If that happens, she could die."

I want to cry. "But it's going to take us forever to carry her out of here."

"Maybe one of us should stay with her," says Marty. "While the other goes for help alone."

I can't bear the thought of going back out in the dark desert alone again. But I also can't bear the thought of staying here with Addie alone. What if she gets worse? What if she dies? "They have to helicopter in here, remember?" I say. "What if they won't come? Or what if they won't come until the morning? What if there's no helicopter nearby? What if they can't find us?"

"Okay, okay," Marty says impatiently. "I just… I don't know what's the right choice here."

"If we take her with us, then an ambulance can come straight to the Flipside. No helicopters. And I really want to stay together right now. We need to stay together."

"I don't know if we can do this, Jolene—carry her all the way out. She was supposed to help guide us on the easier route, but she's barely even conscious. And we have so little water."

"She marked the route on my map. I know where to go."

"What if we get lost? It's going to be dark. There are rattlesnakes."

"I know all this!" I shout, my voice echoing through the quiet mine. "I walked like fifteen miles last night, Marty. And I ran into rattlesnakes and coyotes, and I crashed a bike on the freeway, and I slept all alone on a bench in the middle of nowhere. I can do this!" I say that last line with so much anger and passion and boldness that I surprise even myself. But I know it's true. I know I can get Addie out of this desert. I didn't come all this way to just sit in this mine and watch her die.

Marty's quiet for a while, then, "Okay."

## 26

ADDIE HARDLY ACKNOWLEDGES OUR TYING THE LONG fabric straps across her chest and under her armpits. I take one bar, and Marty grabs the other. "On the count of three," she says, and we lift. Again, the bars fold in on Addie, and I hope she can breathe okay. She's been gasping so much already that it will be hard to tell if the stretcher is causing her even more trouble.

The dim gray rectangle of the mine's doorway guides us out. We set Addie down, and I hope no little cactus pieces or rocks are under her, not that she would probably notice right now. I look up, grateful the moon is slightly bigger than last night.

I wonder how much more light that will give us. A faint orange glow behind the distant mountains tells us where the sun has just set in the west.

I pull out my map and study the route Addie drew. "She said we need to go west around the mine," I tell Marty. "That would be this way."

We pick up the bars and start walking carefully over rocks and around bushes, listening, watching for anything moving, the wheels bouncing over the rocky ground. We can't lift the stretcher at too steep an angle or Addie will slip too much, so Marty basically has to squat as she walks, which must be tiring.

My arms already ache. Because we're concentrating on our steps and gasping for every breath, Marty and I barely speak except for the odd "Watch your step" and "Watch that cactus."

We both sigh with relief every time we put Addie down to check the map. We take sips of water, careful to conserve what we can, but I'm dying of thirst, my heart thumping and head pounding.

I cope with my shaking, aching arms by focusing on the hoot of a nearby owl, the howl of a far-off coyote, the rustling of a bush, which could be anything—a rabbit, lizard, rattlesnake. Suddenly, a cloud of something explodes out of a bush in a burst of wild flapping, startling Marty and me so badly that we both scream in terror.

"Birds," I breathe out. "It's just birds."

"Stupid quail," Marty mutters, like it's the quails' fault for getting scared out of their hiding place by us. "Aw! Cuss nuggets!" she cries out, letting go of her bar, which I quickly grab.

"What?" I ask, setting Addie down gently, which makes my arms shake.

"I backed into something when the birds scared me."

"What?"

"I don't know!" She jumps around on one leg. "Either a cactus or something bit me."

I bend down behind Marty's leg and try to focus in the dim light. A cholla ball is sticking out of her calf, which is a relief. It may be painful, but it's a million times better than a snakebite. "It's cactus," I say. "We have to pull it out somehow."

"With what?" Marty asks. "We can't exactly grab it with our hands."

I study the ground, looking for a couple of rocks to use, but they're all too small. I scan the ground and find a stick under a nearby tree. Its thorns pierce my hand, and I stifle a cry.

I try to scrape the cholla ball off with the stick, but it just crunches along the side of the ball, and Marty shrieks in pain. "I can't get a hold of it," I tell her. "The stupid cactus won't come out."

"And man, that thing hurts," Marty says.

We need something that can go all the way around the cactus, like a belt or strap, something that will grip the cholla ball. I consider taking one of the fabric strips from the stretcher, but then Addie won't be as secure. Instead, I sit down and, my foot screaming in pain, pull off my tight sneaker and remove my sweaty sock.

"What are you doing?" Marty asks, a note of irritation in her voice.

I put my shoe back on and carefully slip one end of the sock around the cholla, the barbed needles snagging the fabric. I pull. Marty shouts as the cactus rips out of her leg.

"Sorry," I say. "But it's out now."

Marty sucks in air. "Yeah, I could tell."

I reach over and feel Addie's forehead. She seems to be working harder than ever to breathe. "She's really hot."

"And probably only getting hotter," Marty says. "Let's move on."

I study the map again before we continue pulling Addie through the dark desert. Finally we hit the trail Addie marked on my map, grateful that we can avoid the cactus more easily now.

Marty walks quietly, which is probably best since I'm breathing so hard from carrying Addie. Unfortunately, though, I'm left with nothing but my thoughts.

*What if we can't find the Flipside Café?*

*What if our stretcher falls apart?*

*What if we run out of water?*

*What if Addie gets sicker?*

I wonder if the explorers I've read about focused on what-ifs.

*What if my boat sinks?*

*What if my camel dies?*

*What if I run into wild animals?*

*What if my motorcycle gets a flat tire?*

*What if my plane crashes?*

Would they have done all the things they did if that was all they thought about? I suppose a person could spend their whole life focusing on the what-ifs of every adventure because there are so, so many.

My muscles cramp. My legs feel like jelly and try to buckle with every step. My aching arms scream for rest. My throat burns for the water that's now gone. Even so, a new what-if has started to creep into my mind. And it's fighting all the other what-ifs. Especially when I see the far-off lights of the Flipside's landing strip.

*What if I actually succeed?*

"I see it," Marty says, and it sounds like she's choking up. "I see lights."

"I see them, too," I say, my heart racing, and not just from dehydration and weariness and fear. There's something new. I can't put my finger on it, but it feels good. It feels hopeful.

"You were right," Marty says, sniffling and laughing. "Thank you, God!" she shouts at the starry sky. "I promise I'll never steal Grandpa's car ever again!"

Now I can't stop myself from smiling. Marty probably had no idea whether Addie and I would be right about the map and the route. For all she knew, we could've ended up wandering the desert until morning. For all she knew, we could've been wandering to our deaths. "Thank you for trusting me," I say, the lights growing brighter with every step. "And thank you for believing in me."

And for the first time in my life, I feel like all kinds of things are possible. Even for me.

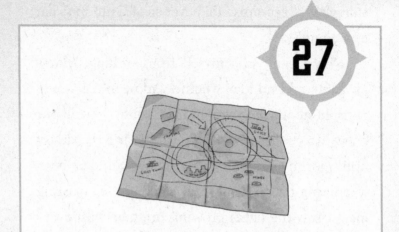

# 27

WE PLACE ADDIE ON THE FLIPSIDE'S CREAKY WOODEN porch, and I find an outside outlet to charge my phone. Marty and I collapse next to Addie, the splintery wood groaning, while I wait for the phone to charge enough to turn on.

"We made it," Marty says, pulling her knees up to her chest, her face in her hands. She presses her forehead to her knees and sucks in a shuddering breath. "This would've killed them," she murmurs to herself. "They couldn't have survived going through it again."

I want to ask her what she means, but the phone

lights up, showing a charge. I immediately dial Addie's mom's phone number.

She answers on the first ring with a frantic "Yes?" Even though it's the middle of the night.

"Mrs. Chapman?" I say.

"Yes. Who's this?"

"My name is Jolene," I tell her. "I'm here with Adelaide."

"Is she okay? Where is she?"

"She's hurt, and we need you to call an ambulance to come to the Flipside Café at Alamo Lake."

"Why is she way out there?" Mrs. Chapman demands. "I want to talk to her."

"I'm sorry. She can't talk," I say. "She's really sick."

Mrs. Chapman is sobbing now. "What's happening?"

"Please call an ambulance, and I promise we'll explain everything. But we need help right now. You can reach me on this number after you call them. Please call now. We don't have any time to waste." I hang up, and my stomach lurches when

I see that I have five voice mails from numbers I don't recognize. My mom? I can't worry about that right now, and I can't bring myself to listen to them.

"She's really upset," I say to Marty.

"She'd be a whole lot more upset if it weren't for you, Jolene." I look at her, and she smiles. "Seriously. Addie wouldn't have survived another day in the sun with her water gone." We both look down at Addie, who seems to be gasping for every breath. "You're the only reason she's alive right now."

I get the same feeling as when I first saw the lights of the Flipside—that *I'm doing it* feeling. The *I've done it* feeling. It makes me feel like I can do a whole lot more—maybe even face Mom when I get home, face her in every way I need to.

"What time is it?" Marty asks.

"It's about two."

"Wow," she whispers. "If we left the mine around eight, then that means it took us six hours to get back here."

"It honestly didn't feel that long when we were walking it," I say. "I just kept focusing on taking one more step instead of thinking about how long we'd been going or had to go."

"That's probably a good tactic," Marty says, sighing, her arms now wrapped around her knees. I hear coyotes off in the distance, and this time I don't think they're zombies. I snort a little.

"What?" Marty asks.

"Nothing. I was just remembering something. I'll tell you about it later." I lift Addie's hot head onto my lap and push her hair back from her forehead. "She feels like a furnace."

The phone rings, and I recognize Mrs. Chapman's number. I answer it, and she immediately starts talking. "They're on their way right now," she says. "They'll have to take her to Wickenburg, and I'm meeting them there. Is she okay? What happened? Why is she there?"

I take a deep breath and do my best to explain everything I can to Mrs. Chapman, who keeps crying and saying things like, "I should've known she was doing this" and "How could I not have known?" and "Please let her be okay."

"She will be okay," I assure her, but we have other calls to make.

As soon as we hang up, I hand the phone to Marty. "You're up," I say. "We really don't have anyone else we can call."

She takes a deep breath. "Just gotta...steel myself for what's coming," she says before dialing her parents.

After a frantic conversation with her mom, who has to come get us, Marty hangs up. "I'm grounded forever," she says.

"I'll tell them everything," I say. "This is all my fault. Maybe it will help."

"Maybe." Her lips turn up a little. "And yes, it is totally all your fault."

We're both so weary from everything that's happened that we doze off on the porch, rousing at the ambulance's siren, which also wakes up most everyone in the RV park. They pour into the dirt parking lot of the café, still in nightgowns and slippers. One old guy is wearing nothing but boxers and a white tank top.

"Did Frank finally die?" someone calls.

"I'm standing right here, woman!" the old guy in boxers shouts back. "I know you can see me!"

Ellie comes running out of a trailer, wrapping a flowery robe around herself. "What on earth?" she says, but there's too much chaos to explain anything as the paramedics rush to Addie.

"She's hurt her legs," I say. "She crashed her ultralight."

"We think she might have an infection," Marty adds. "And really severe heatstroke."

They move her onto a stretcher, securing her head. "Please, step back," a paramedic orders. "We're going to take good care of your friend."

Another paramedic shines a flashlight into Addie's eyes, opening one with his fingers. "Can you hear me?" he asks. "Can you tell us what happened?"

Addie's eyes flutter open, and she starts crying. "Jolene," she croaks through the confusion.

I rush to her and grab her hand. "I'm here," I tell her. "And your mom's going to be at the hospital." Then they wheel her away, my hand slipping from hers, and all I'm left with as they drive away is that look of fear on her face.

"Be brave," I whisper into the darkness, the ambulance speeding down the dirt road, leaving a light trail of dust in their wake. I know Addie *will* be brave, even though I saw how scared she is. And I wonder how it's possible for someone to be so brave and so scared at the same time.

## 28

THE DOOR OF THE FLIPSIDE CAFÉ JINGLES, STARTLING ME awake. After all the chaos of the ambulance, Ellie let us come inside and get some water and wait for Marty's parents—after some explanation, of course. The moment Marty and I sat down at a table, we fell asleep.

Two people who must be Marty's parents stand in front of us. Her mom looks just like her. Marty lifts her own sleepy head, her forehead all red and imprinted with the patterns of her bracelets. She looks at me, then turns slowly in her seat.

Marty's mom crosses her arms, taps her foot— typical angry parent stance. Marty's dad seems more worried, his eyebrows drawn together. They're both wearing mostly pajamas. Marty's mom has on a pair of jean shorts with a partially tucked-in nightgown that has a sleeping giraffe on it, and Marty's dad is wearing pajama pants covered in pictures of hamburgers. They must've left the house quickly.

Marty's mom says, "Martina Elizabeth Abernathy Peterson."

It takes me a moment to realize that's Marty's full name, and it's about the longest name I ever heard in my life. I don't even have a middle name because Mom said middle names are pointless—no one ever uses them. But I guess she was wrong.

"Mom," Marty says tiredly. "I know, okay?"

Marty's mom steps forward, dark eyes flashing with fury, and points at her daughter. "No!" she declares. "You don't know!" Then she bursts into a tirade about Marty's actions and leaving her grandpa's without telling him and taking his car when she doesn't even have her license.

Marty stares at her mom quietly. She doesn't

argue or talk back. She just takes it. The whole time Marty's dad watches her sadly. Eventually, Marty's mom's rage turns into tears, and Marty's dad grabs his wife's hand and pats it.

When her mom is finally done, Marty clears her throat and says softly, "Can I talk to you privately, please?" The three of them walk to a corner of the restaurant, and I watch Marty's lips moving, but she's speaking so quietly I can't hear what she's saying. When she points to me, my stomach does a little flip. Even though I said I'd take the blame, I still wish I knew what she was telling them.

Marty's mom's face gradually softens as Marty continues speaking. She looks from Marty to me and then back to Marty. I want to cry out, *Please talk over here where I can hear you!* but I stay quiet, frustrated, and confused. And I'm tired. So tired I could fall right off this chair. I've never wanted to go back to sleep more in my life. My body shakes with exhaustion.

Marty's mom walks over to me, bends down, and says softly, "Jolene?"

I nod. And then she does something so unexpected that I freeze in my seat, not knowing how
to react. Marty's mom throws her arms around
me and starts crying, which makes me start crying, though I'm not completely sure what we're crying
about. But it feels good to cry with Marty's mom.

Finally she pulls away and tells me, "We'll have
lots of time to talk in the car."

But before we can leave the Flipside, we have
to buy a container of gas and drive it to Marty's
grandpa's car, still stranded on the side of the road.
They decide it will be best for Marty's dad to drive
the car back and stay a day to help his dad, since
Marty "really let him down," as Marty's mom says.
She also doesn't want to drag out getting me home.
I've been gone since Friday evening, and it's Sun-
day morning, the sun just starting to rise.

I don't want to think about Mom, but I can't
stop the questions from nagging me: What did she
do when she found me missing? How long would
she have waited before going to the police? Would
she even go to the police and risk their seeing her as

she is? Risk their coming to our house and finding her pills?

Marty hugs her dad after he pours the gas into her grandpa's car. Then he says goodbye to Mrs. Peterson and looks at me. "It was nice to meet you, Jolene," he says.

I swallow. "Thank you," I say because I'm not really sure what else to say.

"You take care of yourself, okay?" he says, and I nod.

Marty's mom speeds down the road, Marty still sitting in the back with me. "It's safer back here," she whispers.

I smile. My phone rings, but I don't recognize the number or area code. Mrs. Peterson looks at me in the rearview mirror. "You answer that," she orders. "It could be your mom."

I push the answer button with a shaky finger. "Hello?" I say softly.

"Where the heck is my bike?" a man on the other end shouts.

I let out a big breath. "Oh," I gasp. I look at

Marty, and she must have heard the man's shouting because she covers her mouth, holding back a smile. "Oh, I'm so sorry about what I did."

"Well, where is it?" the man demands.

"It's under the Hope sign. You know that little town? It's about twenty miles from Quartzsite."

"Yeah, I know where that is. I sure *hope* it's still there."

"I hid it in a bush. I think it should be okay."

"And what kind of condition is it in? Or dare I even ask?"

I see Mrs. Peterson's questioning eyes in the rearview mirror. I bite my lip. "I'm so sorry. It has a flat tire."

The man's quiet for a while. Then he says in a much calmer, but flat, tone, "Don't worry about it. So did you find your friend or what?"

"Yes," I say. "Yes, I did. Thank you for your help."

"Not like I had any choice in the matter," the man says and hangs up. I turn the ringer off and put the phone away in my bag.

Mrs. Peterson clears her throat. "Care to explain all that, please?"

I nod, and Marty opens her mouth, but Mrs. Peterson snaps her fingers. "No," she says, and I can see where Marty gets her intimidating personality. "From Jolene. I want to hear Jolene's story. The whole thing. From beginning to end."

## 29

TAKING A DEEP BREATH, I BEGIN TO TELL MRS. PETERSON my story. We drive along the empty, winding desert highway, and I don't stop speaking for at least thirty minutes. Just as we're passing the Wenden gas station where I slept on the bench, I finish explaining how we made the stretcher from the ultralight parts.

"I'm very, very concerned about your mom," Mrs. Peterson says.

"Why?" I ask, jerking my head toward her. Did Marty tell her about the pills?

"Why!" Mrs. Peterson declares, like it's the most ridiculous thing she's ever heard. "Why! Because she hasn't heard from you since Friday night. Because she's probably filed a missing persons report. Because she's probably beside herself with worry, and we have absolutely no way of getting in touch with her." Mrs. Peterson shakes her head and clucks her tongue. "Why, indeed."

I gulp. "Sorry," I croak out. "But I don't know that she's all that worried about me. She's... preoccupied."

"Tell me about that," Mrs. Peterson says. "Tell me about your mom."

I look at Marty, and she raises her eyebrows in an encouraging way. "No," I whisper, shaking my head.

Marty grabs my hand again and squeezes it. "Do you trust me?" she asks.

I think of Marty helping me get on the bus. Marty forcing me to go to her grandpa's. Marty hunting me down when I snuck out. Marty going out in the desert with me. When she didn't have to do any of it. "Yes," I say.

Marty says, "You can trust her, too."

But I can't say it. I've been holding it in, hiding

it, for so long that I'm not sure my voice will allow me to say it.

Marty turns to her mom. Her throat moves, like she's swallowing a lot. "We need to tell her about Lucy, Mom," she finally says, her voice breaking.

I can see Mrs. Peterson's eyes in the rearview mirror—big and brown with sadness in the back of them, hidden by a lot of confidence and that take-charge attitude. Just like Marty.

"Who's Lucy?" I ask.

Mrs. Peterson takes a deep breath and says, "Lucy was Marty's sister."

I turn my head to Marty. "Was?"

Marty looks away from me, out the car window, and wipes her cheeks. "Was," she whispers.

"This is a hard story, Jolene," says Mrs. Peterson, her eyes glassy. "Hard for me to tell. Hard for Marty to hear, even though she knows it all. But if it can help someone, then I have to tell it, don't I?" She stares at me in the rearview mirror, like she's waiting for an answer. "Sometimes telling your story is the best thing you can do to help someone," she continues. "Even when the story's not easy. Even when it hurts to tell it."

A tear breaks loose and runs down Mrs. Peterson's cheek. She wipes it away and breathes slowly in and out, like she has to prepare herself for what's to come. And then Mrs. Peterson begins to tell me her story—hers and Marty's dad's and Marty's story. Lucy's story.

She tells me about Lucy getting her wisdom teeth taken out and the surgeon prescribing the same pills that Mom takes—oxycodone. Lucy was addicted after only a week, and when they tried to cut her off, she spent all her savings getting more pills. And when the savings ran out, she resorted to stealing from her family. They got her on a waiting list for a hospital right away, but the lists are long. Too long.

And then while they were waiting, the worst thing that could've happened happened. Lucy tried heroin because it's cheaper than the pills. I shudder as Mrs. Peterson talks about how a person uses a needle to inject themselves. I've read about it online, and I've been watching Mom's wrists, checking her feet from time to time. One day while she was sleeping, I carefully slipped her socks off so I could check between her toes for signs. When I pulled her toes apart, she shot up and cried, "What on earth are you doing, Jolene?" I told her I was giving her a foot massage, but I doubt she was convinced.

"*Once*," Mrs. Peterson forces out, slapping the steering wheel. "That's all it was. One time, and she overdosed."

Marty sniffles, looking away from me. Now I'm the one who reaches over and grabs her hand, folding it in my scraped and bloody fingers.

"Over a hundred people die every day in this country from that horrible drug," Mrs. Peterson says. "And I never thought in a million years my Lucy could be one of them. But it can happen to anyone, Jolene—no matter how rich or poor or where they come from or what color they are. That drug doesn't care. It will take anyone.

"That's why I started a charity. Lucy's Hope. It's to help people going through what we went through, people who maybe don't have enough money to get help and can't wait so long. And that's why Marty's going to be a doctor. Because something like that changes your whole life. It changes how you see the world. It changes your priorities. It can even change who you are."

Mrs. Peterson gazes at me in the rearview mirror, and I turn my head away and say, "I'm sorry." Because I am. So sorry for Lucy. And for Marty. And for their parents. And for the over a hundred every day.

And I'm sorry for myself. And for Mom. And for whatever might happen.

Mrs. Peterson says, "We know what it's like to watch someone get lost in those pills. It doesn't mean they're a bad person. It happens so fast. Maybe they get hurt and don't understand what they're taking before it's too late." She stares at me, her eyes big and expectant. And caring. "Did your mom get hurt, Jolene?"

I nod slowly.

"She got hurt bad, didn't she?"

I nod again, the tears forming so fast, they're already spilling onto my cheeks.

"Jolene," Mrs. Peterson says, reaching her hand back. Marty turns away from the window and grabs her mom's hand. But Mrs. Peterson is looking at me. "You can't help your mom or yourself by hiding it."

Marty finally looks at me, her eyes red and swollen from crying. I open my mouth to speak, and a sort of wail comes out, and then I'm crying so hard that I fall onto the seat, my face in my hands, trying to tuck my legs into myself. Marty takes my head into her lap and rubs her hand over my hair as a mom would do. Or a sister.

And I cry and cry and cry. I cry out all my sadness and worry and exhaustion. But I also cry from relief because suddenly everything feels different. For the first time since the car crash, someone's here to help.

## 30

I WAKE WITH MY HEAD STILL ON MARTY'S LAP. RUBBING MY swollen eyes, I sit up, waking Marty, and see that we're back in Phoenix, not far from my apartment.

"You okay?" Marty asks, yawning.

I nod and pull out Mom's phone, checking for any messages about Addie. There's a voice mail from Mrs. Chapman's phone number.

"Play it on speaker," Marty says.

Mrs. Chapman lets us know that they're at the hospital and Addie has already had X-rays and is on an IV for her heatstroke and dehydration. She's broken both her legs in several places and will need to go in for surgery right away. She says she'll continue to give us updates, then she pauses a moment and adds, "Thank you so much. If there's anything I can possibly do to repay you for this, please let me know." Then she hangs up.

"I hope she's going to be okay," I say, slipping the phone back into my bag.

"Sounds like she will be," Mrs. Peterson reassures us as she turns into the apartment parking lot, which is quiet since some people have probably already left for work and the rest are hiding out from the heat. I guide her to our apartment, and she parks the car. Then she turns around in the driver's seat, reaches out, and touches my arm. "I know this is hard. But you need to go inside and do this."

"She's probably going to be so mad at me," I say.

"Good," says Mrs. Peterson, and I jolt a little. She smiles. "Not because you deserve her anger, but because you'll have her attention. When they totally stop caring...that's when it's the hardest." She takes a deep breath. "Sometimes people get angry when confronted." She grimaces. "More than sometimes. I think maybe it's best you go in first so she doesn't feel overwhelmed. She doesn't know us. I don't want her to feel like she's under attack."

"But what if I say something wrong? Or make things worse?"

Mrs. Peterson nods. "Just be honest, Jolene, and you can't be wrong. Tell her how she's hurting you. She might not even know." She gives me a warm smile. "We'll wait outside until you feel it's okay for us to come in. Just wave us up."

I leave the car and trudge up the old concrete stairway. It's hard to believe the last time I trekked up these steps was after I saw Addie crash. That feels like a lifetime ago.

The door is already unlocked, cracked even, and I push it open. My stomach falls out from under me when I see Mom sitting at our little kitchen table, head down on one outstretched arm, my letter clutched in her hand. Her head shoots up at the sound of the door. Her eyes are red and swollen, her hair matted and tangled.

I slowly close the door and stand in front of it, frozen, my only movement the nonstop quaking of my hands, which settle only a little when I squeeze them together. I don't know what to say to her. I can't find the words. It's as though I've boxed them away like the car-crash feeling.

"I didn't know what to do," Mom finally says, her voice cracking. "I didn't know where you went. I didn't have a phone to call anyone because you took it."

I look down at the dingy carpet. "I'm sorry," I manage to choke out. "Your phone is okay. And I didn't spend very much money."

She stands up, clutching the edge of the table as though she might fall over. "I went to the police yesterday," she says. "But they wouldn't put out an Amber Alert because they said you ran away. I told them you wouldn't run away. That this wasn't like that." Tears run down her cheeks. "I told them you wouldn't run away. They didn't believe me."

Staring down at the carpet, I say, "I didn't run away. I told you I had to go help my friend."

"I thought…" Mom's voice breaks. "I thought maybe you weren't coming back. I don't know what I would do if you didn't come back. You're the only . . ." She stops and looks me over, her eyes wide. "What happened to you?"

I look down at my shredded knees and clothes and hands. "I got in a little accident, but I'm okay. Really," I assure her. "I'm fine. It's just scrapes."

Mom finally lets go of the table and walks over to me. I think she's going to start yelling or maybe shake me, however someone might react when they're at their angriest. But then she swings her arms around me and grips me so hard that my breath catches and my muscles and sunburned skin cry out in pain. "You broke my heart," she says.

A knife stabs right into my chest. "You broke mine, too," I whisper.

"I'm so alone," she says, crying now.

"You're not alone," I say. "I'm here with you."

She cries a long time before pulling away from me and wiping the tears from my own cheeks. "Where have been?" she demands. "What have you done?"

"It's a long story," I say. "And there are some people outside."

She startles a little. "What people?"

"They're my friends. They've helped me a lot over the last couple of days. I don't know what I would've done without their help."

Mom stiffens up. "Are they this girl's family? The girl you went to help? Is she okay?"

"Yes, I think she's going to be okay. But they're not her family. They brought me home. They want to meet you."

Mom pushes her hair back from her face and rubs her nose, her eyes scanning our grimy apartment. "Jolene, I don't know if I'm up for meeting anyone right now. And the apartment is such a mess. I'd rather clean up first."

But I think it has to happen now. There will always be excuses. "Please," I say to her. "They've done so much. They're nice people. Please, will you meet them?"

Mom wipes her hands on her gray sweats, then smooths down the front of her wrinkled T-shirt, letting out a big sigh. "If it's that important to you, then okay."

I step outside the apartment and wave down to Mrs. Peterson in the car. She nods, and she and

Marty get out. They meet me in the doorway. "Everything okay?" Marty whispers in my ear.

"I hope so," I say.

Mom wrings her hands and continues smoothing her T-shirt as we all three step into the living room together. "Mom," I tell her. "This is my friend, Marty. And this is Mrs. Peterson."

"Paula," Mrs. Peterson says, sticking out her hand.

Mom shakes it but doesn't say anything. I can see how nervous and confused and embarrassed she is. She motions toward the couch. "Do you want to sit down?"

Mom and Mrs. Peterson sit on the couch, while Marty and I sit on the floor next to them. I'd give anything to just flop over and go to sleep on the carpet, but this is too important.

"I'm so sorry for how I look," Mom says, giving them a trembling smile. "I've been in quite a state since Jolene went missing."

Mrs. Peterson nods understandingly. "Of course you have. Any mother would be."

"So...where are you all from?" asks Mom.

"Nearby," says Mrs. Peterson. "A few miles away."

"And how did Jolene meet Marty?" asks Mom.

Marty speaks up now. "On the Greyhound. She was trying to get on as an unaccompanied minor." She gives me a goofy look, and I can't help but smile.

Mom's mouth drops open. "You took a Greyhound bus? Where?"

"Just to Quartzsite," I say softly. "Not far."

Mom shakes her head and rubs her blotchy forehead. "I hate to ask what that cost." Then she looks at Mrs. Peterson. "You must think I'm such an irresponsible mother."

"No, I don't think that," says Mrs. Peterson. "But all that really matters is what Jolene thinks." She looks at me, her eyes urging me to speak, but my throat is closed up.

Mom looks at me and then back at Mrs. Peterson and then back at me. She seems to be waiting for someone to say something.

"I feel like I got to know Jolene a bit on the drive

here," says Mrs. Peterson. "I think she would like to say some things to you."

Mom looks at me nervously. "What kind of things?" she asks, squeezing her sweatpants in balled-up fists.

I breathe hard, my stomach as clenched up as mom's fists. This is difficult. Really difficult. "Mom," I finally say. "I think we need help. Your pills—"

Mom rockets to her feet. "I don't want to do this in front of strangers, Jolene," she says quickly.

I look at Marty, then turn back to Mom. "They're not strangers, Mom. And I'm tired of being alone. I want them here. And I want to do this now." *Before I lose my nerve*, I don't add. "We can trust them."

Mom breathes heavily, her eyes floating around the room like she doesn't know what to focus on right now. "How do I know that? I just met them."

Mrs. Peterson looks up at Mom. "We lost our Lucy to heroin," she says gently.

Mom looks totally appalled, her eyes darting to Mrs. Peterson. "I don't *do* heroin," she says.

And I'm hugely relieved to hear it. And by how

angry Mom is, I'm tempted to believe her, though I also know that addicts can lie a lot.

We're all quiet until Mom finally sits back down, breathing hard, tears filling her eyes again. "I would never do heroin," she says, wiping her eyes with a trembling hand. "*Never.*"

Mrs. Peterson nods. "It doesn't make someone a bad person. My Lucy was a good girl," she says, nodding and sniffing. "So caring. So thoughtful. The drug can't change that."

Mom sits up straighter. "It's fine," she says. "It won't ever come to that. It's not even *close* to that. I can stop when I want to. I'll just stop. So...you can go now. We appreciate your concern, but we'll be fine."

I stand up in front of Mom. Looking down at her, I say, "No, I don't think you can stop that easily."

Mom's eyes widen. "Jolene, I can too stop."

"No, you can't," I say, my eyes overflowing. "Or you won't."

"I can, and I will," Mom insists.

"Then why haven't you already?" I ask. "It's

been two years. Why haven't you stopped? You don't want to."

Mom shakes her head frantically. "Yes, I do. I swear, Jolene."

"Then do it," I say. "Throw them all in the toilet."

Now Mom looks really scared. "I will."

"Do it now," I say. "Right now."

Mom runs a trembling hand through her messy hair. "I just need to plan. I need to plan for it. That's all."

I grit my teeth, clench my fists. "You won't. You won't even try."

"You don't understand, Jolene," Mom says. "I *have* tried. Several times. It's really painful."

"Then you just need some help," I say.

"No, you don't understand," she says again, squeezing the bridge of her nose. She probably feels like no one in the world understands right now, but I remember the over a hundred every day. "I've tried. The insurance company has been horrible."

I'm shocked to hear that Mom has tried to get

help already. Even calling the insurance? And they wouldn't help her?

"After a while it feels pointless," Mom says. "Like no one cares. So why should I?"

"I care," I say.

"I don't know what to do," Mom says. "I think I could've stopped a long time ago if I'd had help. But there's no one. No one wants to help."

And I realize right now that Mom sounds like me. Or I've been sounding like Mom. "Mrs. Peterson runs a charity," I tell her. "It's to help people like us. But will you take the help?" Maybe I've felt like I've been on my own forever, like no one would help me. But here they are now, wanting to help. And I would never, ever turn it down. I hope Mom won't either.

Mom looks away from me, from all of us, not speaking, her lip quivering. She doesn't seem to want to answer.

"Look at your daughter," Mrs. Peterson says after sitting quietly for the longest time. She let me do all the talking. Maybe that's how it needed to be.

Mom moves her eyes to Mrs. Peterson. She

seems confused for a moment, then looks at me. I wipe my cheeks, not wanting her to see me crying. I want to be strong for her. But I remember Marty crying in the car. And I remember Addie crying. And I think maybe crying doesn't mean you're not strong. Maybe it doesn't mean you're a crybaby. Maybe it takes courage sometimes to show people your tears.

"Do you see how much she cares? How much she loves you?" says Mrs. Peterson.

Mom nods, tears running down her cheeks. "I love her, too."

"She believes in you," says Mrs. Peterson.

Mom reaches out and grabs my hand, then pulls me to her, taking me into her arms. She says, "And I believe in her."

Because sometimes, in order to do what's hardest, the most important thing you need is simply knowing there's someone who believes you can do it.

## 31

# NOW

### BLIPSTREAM DIRECT MESSENGER

**Addie Earhart:** This itching is driving me bananas. It's like they planted mosquito eggs under my casts. I think there's a whole mosquito city under there! How's everything?

**JoJo12:** Good. My mom left for the treatment center day before yesterday.

**Addie Earhart:** So you're at Marty's house now?

**JoJo12:** Yeah.

**Addie Earhart:** When can you go see your mom?

**JoJo12:** Not until she's done with the worst of the detox, so probably like a week.

**Addie Earhart:** What's detox?

**JoJo12:** It's basically getting all the drugs out of her system. They said she'll be very sick while she does it.

**sMarty:** Hi, Addie!

**Addie Earhart:** Hi, Marty! So I guess you got a new phone?

**sMarty:** Yep. And this one is not going in the toilet. Probably.

**Addie Earhart:** So how's it been having Jolene there?

**sMarty:** She drinks the last soda and keeps me up at night asking existential questions.

**JoJo12:** Your mom said I could have the soda. And I don't know what existential means!

**sMarty:** Do you think there are no accidents? How can I change the world? Can the world be changed? It's exhausting!

**Addie Earhart:** Haha!

**Addie Earhart:** Are you guys still there?

**Addie Earhart:** Hello?

**JoJo12:** We're back. I had to kick Marty's butt.

**sMarty:** Lies, all lies. She's a skinny shrimp.

**JoJo12:** A skinny shrimp who carried Addie across the desert.

**Addie Earhart:** Do I have to be reminded of that every five seconds?

**sMarty:** The answer to that question is YES.

**Addie Earhart:** How's the support group?

**JoJo12:** It's good. Everyone is so nice.

**Addie Earhart:** You start school tomorrow like me, right?

**JoJo12:** Yeah, we both do.

**Addie Earhart:** Have a great first day!

**JoJo12:** You too! See you later, Aviator!

**Addie Earhart:** After a while, hodophile!

**sMarty:** WHAT did you just call her??

**Addie Earhart:** Hodophile! It's a person who loves to travel. An adventurer 😊

**JoJo12:** That one's my favorite.

⌒⌒

Marty and I stand on the sidewalk in front of my new middle school, just outside a large open metal gate. Several buses pull into the parking lot in a long yellow line. An endless stream of kids pours through the gate from the surrounding neighborhoods, most of them staring at their phones and wearing earbuds.

I'm frozen, unable to make myself cross the barrier between here and school property. I shift from foot to foot in Marty's old blue flip-flops and smooth the front of the T-shirt she gave me. It says, T-SHIRTS THAT SAY STUFF ARE STUPID.

"You're wearing my lucky T-shirt," Marty says. "The day is going to go great."

I look down at the blue T-shirt. "How is it lucky?" I ask, wiping sweat from my forehead. I wish it weren't still so hot. I'm worried I'll get sweat stains under my arms.

Marty smiles. "It's ironic."

"I don't know what that means."

"People will notice it," she says. "It's funny. In a good way." She gazes around at all the middle schoolers. "They're nervous, too, you know."

"Not nearly as nervous as I am," I say.

She looks at me. "I know you're scared, but you are one of the bravest people I have ever met. You can do this."

"How can someone be brave and scared at the same time?"

Marty tilts her head. "How can someone be brave if they're *not* scared? You can take whatever they throw at you, Jolene."

My eyes move back to the looming gray cinderblock buildings as a muffled voice booms over a loudspeaker. Then a bell rings. I glance at the kids pouring into the school, and my heart pounds.

"Okay," I say, drawing in a deep breath, mentally preparing myself. "I'll see you later, *Martina*."

Marty grins. "Hey, I like my name." She flexes her arms, and she actually does have pretty good muscles. "It means 'warlike.'"

"I like it, too," I say. "I think you could win any battle."

"And you're going to win this one today."

"I hope you're right," I say, smiling and covering my mouth.

Marty reaches up and gently pulls my hand down. "And maybe you could do it without covering your smile. It's a good one. You should show it off." When I don't say anything back, she adds, "You know, I'm glad I dropped my phone in the toilet."

I finally find the courage to smile a little, keeping my hands at my sides. "Me too," I say. Because I really couldn't imagine what my life would be like right now if she hadn't. I think about something Mrs. Peterson has told me—that there are no accidents. Like everything that happened was all leading to this moment right now as I take another deep breath and step through the gate of my new middle school, keeping my head down, wishing I had a phone to stare at instead of my blue flip-flops. Mom came with me last week to find all my classes before she left for the treatment center, so at least I know where I'm heading.

A boy walks by, bumping into me. He stops. "Hey," he cries out, and my stomach jumps. I breathe in slowly, telling myself, *Whatever he's about to say, it's not true. You can take whatever they throw at you, Jolene.*

"Your shirt!" he says, flashing me a mouthful of metal braces.

I breathe out and look down at my T-shirt. "It's ironic," I say softly.

"It's funny! Where'd you get it?"

I look up at him. He has paper-straight brown hair parted in the middle and a smattering of pimples across his pale forehead. "My friend gave it to me," I say. "I think she got it online."

His overgrown hair falls into his eyes, and he pushes it back, once more flashing those braces. "I'm totally ordering one. Twinsies!" he says, walking away. After several steps, he turns and smiles at me again. I smile back. I do not cover my mouth.

I head on to my first class of the day, still smiling, still not covering my mouth, as I step through the door. For once I don't feel annoyed about Marty being such a know-it-all.

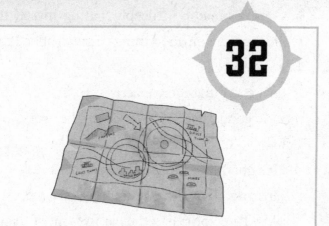

## 32

I STARE OUT THE CAR WINDOW, WATCHING STRIP MALLS gradually change to homes as we get farther into the suburbs. This is going to be hard, but I can face it. I feel a light punch on my arm and look over at Marty. She smiles. Her parents are talking softly up front, holding hands over the center console. This is going to be hard for them, too.

Marty is giving me an expectant look, so I smile back to show I'm okay. But when Mr. Peterson slows the car, the car-crash feeling comes. I don't box it up anymore. I don't need all that heavy storage weighing me down, cluttering my insides. Besides, the car-crash feeling never stops coming anyway. I breathe in deeply, letting myself feel it while focusing on good things instead of bad things I can't control.

It's good that mom's here.

It's good that she's through the worst of the detox.

It's good that I'm going to see her today.

It's good that she'll be happy to see me.

Mr. Peterson parks the car in front of the treatment center, which is just a regular house in the middle of a regular neighborhood. It's not a fancy place—the building is older and stuccoed a light brown, like most other houses in Phoenix. But the paint looks new, and the grass is freshly mowed, and the rose bushes are trimmed. It's not fancy, but it looks homey. And most important, it's what our insurance will cover, after a lot of phone calls and paperwork and waiting, all of which Mrs. Peterson's charity helped us with.

Mom will only be here for four weeks. My instinct is to focus on the negative—to tell myself that's not nearly enough time, that Mom is probably going to relapse. Things I can't control. Even if they're probably true, I decide to tell myself other things.

This is a good start.

This is the biggest step Mom has ever taken.

Anything can happen in the future.

Worrying won't change what's going to happen.

The four of us walk quietly down the concrete walkway, and Marty grabs my hand. Mrs. Peterson knocks on the front door, painted the same color as the rest of the house. A young guy in green scrubs answers and lets us in after we tell him who we're visiting.

We sign in at a little desk in the entryway, then the guy in green scrubs leads us down a tiled hallway to a small room with two twin beds and a chair, where Mom is sitting. She has her hands folded in her lap, like she's been waiting for us.

I don't know what I was expecting, but I know I wasn't expecting her to look like this. She's incredibly pale, and her eyes have such dark rings that they look like little caves. Despite how hot it is outside, she's wearing a big, baggy blue sweater and jeans that hang on her bony body. She's even skinnier than the last time I saw her. She looks like she's been through torture. I guess she has been.

She stands up and gives me a big hug, kissing the top of my head. "Gosh, I've missed you," she says, her voice shaking.

I slowly lift my arms and wrap them around her sharp edges. "I've missed you, too," I tell her, burying my head in her fuzzy sweater, which soaks up my tears.

When she finally releases me, she wipes her eyes and shakes hands with Mr. Peterson. "It's good to see you," he says.

Then she puts out her hand for Mrs. Peterson, who instead throws her arms around Mom. "How are you feeling?" Mrs. Peterson asks.

Mom pulls away and gives us all a weak smile. "Oh, you know..." She sniffs. "It's pretty bad. This sickness." She nods and whispers, "Pretty bad."

Mrs. Peterson holds Mom by the shoulders. "You're through the worst of it. We're so proud of you."

Mom sniffs again. "I don't know that I've done anything to be proud of."

"Nonsense," Mrs. Peterson snaps, and she reminds me so much of Marty right now. "You've done one of the hardest things a person can go through. It's a huge accomplishment."

We make our way out to the living room, where chairs have been set up. People start appearing from the other bedrooms and hallways, and a few others show up at the door. We all sit quietly, waiting for everyone to take their seats.

After almost all the chairs have been filled, a man stands up. "Thanks for coming, everyone. We're so glad to have friends and family here today. Please feel free to introduce yourselves and share whatever is in your heart today, even if that's only your name. That's okay."

The man takes a deep breath. "My name is Brian, and I'm an opioid addict. I have been an opioid addict for nearly twenty years. Rock bottom for me was being found dead at the bottom of a flight of stairs I'd fallen down after shooting heroin laced with fentanyl. They managed to revive me, and I overdosed only six more times after that."

There are sad smiles and nods all around,

understanding smiles and nods, but I gape at Brian. *Six* more times? After overdosing and nearly dying? How could someone do that to themselves?

Brian looks at me and smiles. "Seven times the charm, right? I haven't used now in three years. So you see, it's possible to get better. It feels impossible while you're living it." He chokes up. "But it's possible to break free." He sits back down.

The room is quiet, everyone glancing around at one another, wondering who will be brave enough to stand up next. Mrs. Peterson suddenly stands up. "Hello," she says. "My name is Paula." She takes a deep breath, holding out her hands to Marty and Mr. Peterson. They put their hands in hers and gaze up at her, eyes wide and shining. "We lost our sweet Lucy to a heroin overdose three years ago. I just want to say I admire you all for being here and doing what you need to do to get better. For yourselves. And for the people who love you."

She seems like she wants to say more, but she chokes on the words when she opens her mouth. She manages to get out, "We're honored to be here." Mrs. Peterson sits back down. Marty puts an arm around her mom and leans her head on her shoulder while Mr. Peterson pats her back. I've gotten to know Mr. Peterson better while staying at Marty's, and he's a quiet man, so I'm not surprised he doesn't stand up.

Mom reaches out and grabs my hand. She looks at me, her eyes filled with fear. I can see how scared she is, so I know how brave she's being when she stands up.

We all give her our full attention. She squeezes my hand like she needs it for support—like she needs it to help hold her up. I sit up straight and sturdy, lending her all my strength.

"My name is Madeline," she finally says to the group, even though she's only looking at me, her eyes filled with tears. "And I'm an opioid addict."

# 33

# NOW

### BLIPSTREAM DIRECT MESSENGER

**Addie Earhart:** The air show is tomorrow, and I'm so excited I could scream! Do you think we'll get to meet Joanie Cash? What if she doesn't come? What if she's too old?

**JoJo12:** Never! She seems so young for her age!

**Addie Earhart:** Lol! How would you know that?

**JoJo12:** Oh, just videos and stuff I've seen 😊

**Addie Earhart:** How's school going?

**JoJo12:** School is school. I can tell some of the kids are kind of impressed when they see me walking to school with Marty, though.

**sMarty:** Yep. I exude coolness.

**JoJo12:** Actually, I think they're scared of her.

**sMarty:** As they should be.

**JoJo12:** How's school for you, Addie?

**Addie Earhart:** It's kind of hard to get around in my wheelchair.

**sMarty:** Yeah, if only you hadn't stolen a plane, crashed it, and broken both your legs.

**Addie Earhart:** Everyone at school wants to know what happened to me, and when I tell them how I crashed the ultralight, they think I'm pretty hard-core.

**sMarty:** Everybody loves a rebel. Doesn't anyone want to know how school is going for me?

**Addie Earhart:** Of course!

**sMarty:** My evil plan is working out perfectly. I almost have them all under my control.

**Addie Earhart:** You're so weird, Marty.

**sMarty:** Thank you.

**Addie Earhart:** How's your mom, Jo?

**JoJo12:** We just went for another visit. She looked better. Healthier. Happier.

**Addie Earhart:** Does that mean all the hard stuff is over?

**JoJo12:** No. But at least I won't be going through the hard stuff alone anymore.

The crowd roars with applause as Joanie Cash rolls her plane above us. "You know," Addie says, pointing at the sky from her wheelchair. "That's actually called an aileron roll, even though everyone calls it a barrel roll."

"It's so cool," I say.

"I could totally do that," says Marty. We're sitting in the grass, side-by-side on an old quilt Mrs. Chapman brought.

Mrs. Peterson, arms crossed, looks down at Marty. "Don't even think about it."

Marty laughs. "Sheesh. It's not like I'm Addie."

"Hey!" cries Addie, rolling her wheelchair over our quilt, bunching it up a bit. "I don't think I'll be doing that for a while."

"A long while," says Mrs. Chapman, and she and Mrs. Peterson give each other knowing mom looks.

We all watch as Joanie Cash makes her way back to the ground after her final tricks of the day. "I'm so glad we came," I say, leaning back on my elbows. The sun is shining as always, but the weather has finally cooled down a bit and a nice breeze is blowing. The air smells like plane exhaust and hot dogs and freshly cut grass. "This is amazing."

Joanie Cash lands and drives her plane down the runway. Marty and I stand up and try to get a look at her getting out of the plane. Joanie jumps to the ground like she's far younger than her nearly eighty years. She pulls off her goggles and helmet—one of those old-fashioned leather ones—and waves a hand at the crowd. Everyone claps and cheers.

We fold up the quilt and put our leftover picnic food in the cooler Mrs. Peterson brought. Then we get in line with everyone else who wants to meet

Joanie, get her autograph, or take pictures with her. When we finally reach her, Addie cries out, "Oh my gosh I'm your biggest fan!"

Joanie laughs. "Really? And what's your name?

"Adelaide Chapman. I've even written you fan letters!"

"Oh, yes," Joanie says. "I know that name. Thank you for your letters." Then Joanie turns her attention to me and Marty and tilts her head a little. "Well, hello again."

Addie's mouth drops open. Her eyes dart from me to Marty and back. *"Again?"* she says.

"Bertha and Olga, right?" Joanie says. "How could I forget those names?"

Everyone gives us confused looks. "Um, yeah," Marty says through a nervous laugh. "Those are not actually our real names."

Joanie acts surprised, but it's clearly that—an act. "You don't say?" she says, smirking. "But they're such typical names for young girls these days."

I smile and say, "Hi, Joanie. I'm Jolene, and that's Marty."

"Wait a minute," says Addie, waving her arms frantically in the air. "Do you guys *know* each other?"

"We only met once," I say.

Marty pats Addie on top of her head. "We'll tell you about it later, daredevil."

"I can't wait until later!" Addie cries.

"You had a beautiful hand-drawn map," Joanie says to me, ignoring Addie's hysterics. "It looked like you were searching for something. Have you found it yet?"

I look at our group before turning back to Joanie. "Yes. I did."

Joanie nods. Then she says to all of us, "Wait up while I do my thing, will you?" Then Joanie turns to the others in the crowd. When she's done signing all the things and taking all the pictures, she looks over at us and waves a hand. "Well, come on now. I don't have all day."

I glance around at the others, not sure what Joanie's talking about. Mrs. Chapman smiles down at me. "She's talking to you, Jolene."

"What do you mean?" I ask.

"You're going up with her," Mrs. Chapman says.

"Up where?" I ask.

Joanie laughs. "Where do you think, little girl? We're going up *there*." She points toward the sky. "Let's get to it."

"Go, Jolene! Go!" Addie cries.

Marty pushes me toward Joanie. "Go, go, go!"

"But," I stare at Addie, "it should really be you if someone gets to go."

Addie shakes her head. "Nah! I've had tons of time in the air. It's your turn."

"Just stinking go, Jolene!" Marty cries.

I turn to Mrs. Chapman. "I don't understand. Did you set this up?"

She smiles. "It was your mom's idea. She wanted it to be a really special day for you." Mrs. Chapman had called Mom after they got home from the hospital to thank her for everything and to offer to repay any money I'd spent getting to Addie. They've even started sort of becoming friends, and I'm glad. Mom hasn't had any good friends for a while now.

My throat tightens up, and I swallow. "But how?" I ask. "How could she…"

Mrs. Chapman runs her hand over Addie's hair. "Addie and I may have chipped in." She laughs. "I mean it was the *least* we could do."

Addie makes an exaggerated frown. "And it's not like I have to use all my allowance for gas anymore."

I smile at her. "Thank you," I mouth, and she brightens.

"So are we going or not?" Joanie calls back to us, already halfway to her plane.

I rush up behind her, thinking about Mom. Maybe I won't ever be able to stop the bad thoughts from coming, but I can come up with new ways to answer them.

This is really hard, but *Mom is trying.*

Mom might take pills again, but *she wants to stay well. She can try again.*

This battle takes a lot of her energy and attention away from me, but *that doesn't mean she doesn't love me.*

Mom is going through the hardest thing, but *she's still thinking about me.*

"Throw that on your head, *Jolene*," Joanie orders, handing me a helmet.

I slip it over my head. "Yeah, um, sorry about that—the lying I mean."

Joanie adjusts my helmet straps. "What's that, Bertha?"

I cringe. "It's kind of a complicated story."

"Maybe one day you can tell me about it," she says, buckling me into the passenger seat. "I have a feeling it's quite the exciting story."

"Well, now that you say it, I guess it is kind of an exciting story."

"A real adventure, huh?"

"Yeah." I smile and nod. "An adventure." I glance around the cockpit. "So what kind of plane is this?"

"It's an Extra 330 LX." She tightens my buckles until I feel snug in my seat. "It's strong and light and can go over two hundred miles per hour."

"Wow. Are we going to go that fast?"

Joanie slips the old leather helmet over her own head and puts her goggles on. "We're going to go pretty fast." She climbs into the pilot's seat, and the glass hood closes over us. "But don't worry. I won't do anything too scary. No rolls or flips."

"I'll be disappointed if you don't." I take in a deep breath. "I feel ready for anything."

"I believe you are," Joanie declares. "Challenge accepted."

The engines roar, and we drive around in a circle until we're at the start of the runway. "Here we go," Joanie announces.

In seconds, we're racing down the runway faster than I've ever gone in my life. About to go somewhere I've never been in my life. About to see things I've never seen in my life. We lift up into the clear blue desert sky, my friends, my mom, and the whole city of Phoenix with the vast desert surrounding it far below.

And endless possibilities above.

# AUTHOR'S NOTE

I remember this one day when I was young. My dad stopped in a parking lot somewhere. I can't remember where. The location isn't the important part of this story. What I do remember is him opening up the center console and removing an orange pill bottle. I remember him popping a couple of pills into his mouth and then putting the pill bottle back in the console before getting out of the car. I remember opening the console and taking out the pill bottle. I had just barely read the name on it when he was back in the car, snatching it out of my hands. He threw it in the console and slammed the cover down angrily, slapping it as though to say, *Don't you dare ever do that again.*

I didn't have access to the internet back then, but I never forgot the name on that bottle: hydrocodone. It would be several more years before I would come to understand that my father was an opioid addict. I already knew he was an alcoholic because that's not as easily hidden. I don't remember a moment in my childhood when my father wasn't on some kind of drug, and his behavior when he was in the throes of his addictions...Let's just say it was not okay.

My dad never did recover when I was a child, and I found myself dealing with his addictions even as an adult. One day he called me, demanding that I take him to the doctor because he needed his prescription. He always used intimidation to get what he wanted, but I wasn't a child anymore. And on this day, I finally found the strength to say no and hang up the phone, though it would be several more years before I allowed myself to feel true freedom.

So if you are a child living with an addict, I want you to know that I *do* see you. My heart reaches out to yours to let you know that you are not alone. I know that it sometimes feels like things will never get better, like *they* won't ever get better. I hope they will. Maybe they won't. But you need to know that your joy and peace will not always depend on their sobriety. One day, you, too, will be fully grown and you will be able to say no and hang up the phone. There's no shame in that—no shame in protecting your heart and your mental health and your well-being. No shame in finding your own freedom.

I would like to say a quick thank-you to my literary agent, Shannon Hassan; my editor, Lisa Yoskowitz; and everyone else at Little, Brown Books for Young Readers who worked on this book. Thank you to all my friends and family who have supported me and to the many booksellers and educators who work every day to care for our children in a multitude of ways. Many of them will only read this book because an educator or bookseller handed it to them. Thank you to God, who shows me time and time again that some good can come out of even the worst things.

But most of all, thank you to the child reading

this story. You kept me motivated to continue writing this book during a very dark and disappointing year when I've never felt less creative. It was the thought that you, the child living with an addict, would one day read this story that gave me the determination to keep going when at times all I wanted to do was throw my hands up and forget about the world and all my responsibilities.

So thank *you*. I see you.

# DISCUSSION QUESTIONS

1. Jolene observes, "It's pretty cool to discover something, even if it's something small. Even if I'm not the first person to discover it" (p. 4). Why is the act of discovery so exciting? What is something you discovered this year?

2. Jolene gets frustrated when adults won't listen to her. Why do you think grown-ups sometimes dismiss kids or don't believe them?

3. Why does Jolene try to hide the truth about her mom's addiction to painkillers? Is she protecting her mom, herself, or both?

4. Marty offers the advice, "Keeping secrets doesn't always help people. Sometimes you need to tell the truth to help them" (p. 90). When should you keep a secret, and when should you tell it?

5. In one of her BlipStream messages, Addie says, "I belong in the sky" (p. 168). Where do you feel like you most belong?

6. The novel moves across Arizona, from the city of

Phoenix to the small town of Quartzsite and the desert of Alamo Lake—and back again. If you live in Arizona or have visited any of these sites, how do you feel reading about places you have experienced? If you haven't been to them, how does the author help you imagine Arizona?

7. Marty doesn't believe anyone is actually lost in the desert, yet she helps Jolene anyway. Why?

8. Mrs. Peterson says, "Sometimes telling your story is the best thing you can do to help someone" (p. 264). Why might someone not want to tell their story? How can finding the courage to tell your story help other people? How can it help you?

9. Why does it matter that Jolene's mom looks directly at Jolene when she says at group therapy, "I'm an opioid addict" (p. 295)?

10. What three words would you use to describe Jolene? How do you think Jolene would describe herself? How do her big adventure and new friendships change how she sees herself?

11. In her author's note, Dusti Bowling shares why she wrote this novel and how you, the reader, inspire her. Why does being seen by others who have had similar experiences matter? How is Jolene truly seen by Marty?

Turn the page for a sneak peek of

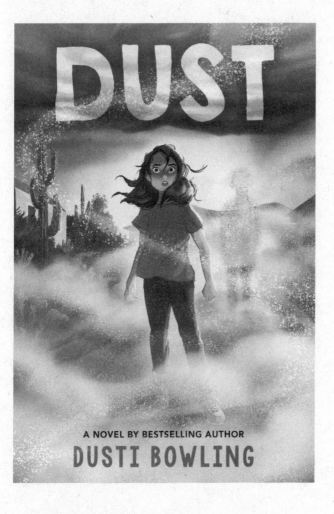

**AVAILABLE AUGUST 2023**

# Prologue.

*P-R-O-L-O-G-U-E.*

**Prologue.**

I was a toddler the first time I almost died. We were living in Oklahoma, and the air was so humid, we could barely see our neighbor's house. At least that's what my parents tell me. I don't remember because I was only two.

Humidity that thick is like steam rising off a bubbling witch's brew made of several ingredients: mold, pollen, ragweed, smoke, and dust. Pollution stew. It all hangs suspended in the heavy air, making my airways tighten so that I cough because I feel like I'm breathing air mud. Or sky slime. Or spaghetti sauce. Basically imagine trying to breathe sludge, and that's how I feel during an asthma attack. Then throw a big boulder on your chest and shove a stone down your throat.

I was having a hard time breathing that day ten years ago, so Mom gave me an extra treatment while Dad was at work. She kept my inhaler in her pocket, where one has been ever since. She hadn't showered in days, afraid of leaving my side for even five minutes, but I seemed to be doing all right after using the nebulizer. I was giggling at Elmo on TV. She didn't hear any wheezing, so she went to wash off three days of worry and sweat and anxiety.

It only takes a few minutes for a person to suffocate.

When Mom came out, hair still dripping wet, a towel wrapped around her middle, she thought I was asleep. But my fingernails were blue, and she couldn't get me to wake up.

She called 911, then picked me up and sprayed my inhaler into my mouth, but it can't get into your lungs when your whole airway is swollen shut. Then she did mouth-to-mouth until the paramedics showed up.

I spent three days in the hospital recovering from that asthma attack.

Mom and Dad decided we had to leave Oklahoma after that. They asked the doctors where we should go. They wanted to know where I could breathe the best. The doctors told them a lot of people take their kids to Arizona, where it's dry, the allergens are low, and freezing winds don't blow. Of course, the one downside of the desert is dust, so my parents chose the least windy place they could find—Clear Canyon City, a town surrounded by mountains that block the wind, making the air still and clear.

My parents have always told me that every breath I take is precious because I so easily could have stopped breathing at two years old. Breath is important, maybe the most important thing in the world. We can't live without it for more than a few minutes. Breath is powerful. We can't speak without it. My parents also tell me that what I choose to do with my breath can change the world. What will I do with all these breaths I may not have had?

Well, I've been able to breathe pretty well for the last ten years, though I can't say I've done anything super important with those breaths—mostly a lot of talking with my two best friends and spelling every spelling bee word in existence and bickering with my parents about my room being a "pigsty."

It's amazing how little we think about our

breath when it comes easily. Of course, I still have to use my inhaler and sometimes even do a breathing treatment when the wind becomes too intense for the mountains to block and the dust swirls. But it's been manageable.

Until now.

Until Adam came to Clear Canyon City with his downcast eyes and quiet voice and horrible dark secrets.

And the dust.

It was like he brought the dust with him. And now all I can think about is breath.

# chapter 1

**Portentous.**
*P-O-R-T-E-N-T-O-U-S.*
**Portentous.**

On Saturday morning at 9:32, all three of our phones screeched the warning at the same time. I wasn't allowed to have my phone at the kitchen table, so it was shrieking on the counter nearby. Mom and Dad picked theirs up because *they* were apparently allowed to have phones at the kitchen table. Parents could be hypocritical like that. Or as Dad would say, *As supreme ruler of the universe, I'm allowed to do what I want.*

Mom dropped her forkful of buckwheat pancake,

her face filled with both surprise and confusion. "Dust storm?"

"In Phoenix?" I asked.

Dad slowly shook his head, studying his own phone, his eyebrows drawn together. "It says Clear Canyon City."

The three of us all looked at one another before jumping out of our chairs and hurrying to the kitchen window, hands and noses pressed against the glass, searching for the dust. The air was growing hazy, which *was* sort of strange for this time of year. It definitely got a little dusty around here every now and then, especially when the big monsoon storms hit, but this time of year was usually nice and clear.

I turned to Dad, who had his lips pursed and eyes squinted. Individual strands of his gray-speckled brown hair were beginning to rise and stand up. Lifting my hand from the glass, I pointed at his head. "Whoa. Your hair." Then I saw that Mom's longer blond strands were starting to hover as well. I touched a finger to her bare freckled arm, and a spark of electricity shocked both of us. I yelped and snatched my hand away.

"Ouch!" She rubbed her arm and shot me an accusing look, as though I'd deliberately attacked her with electrical powers. Then Dad reached over and touched my arm, zapping me again, and we all burst into a sort of nervous laughter.

"What in the world?" Mom said as she and Dad rushed out the front door to see what else they could see. "Avalyn, get your butt back in that house," Mom ordered when she saw me following them. Yeah, she could be pretty bossy. If Dad was the supreme ruler, then she was the *supremer* ruler. I probably should've listened, though. To say that dust was hard on my lungs would be an understatement. It didn't help that we'd had almost no rain in a year. The desert dirt had become as fine and dry as the powdered sugar sprinkled over my buckwheat pancakes that morning.

The three of us stood side by side in our front yard, mouths open, gaping at the wall of light brown. It was like a gigantic, muddy, frothy wave crashing toward us in slow motion. Mom reached into her pocket and pulled out the inhaler she always carried, even when I wasn't with her. I guess it probably made her feel better—like as long as she carried it, I would always be safe no matter what. Dad carried one, too.

Mom passed me the inhaler, and when her hand brushed mine, it was as though her wonder, confusion, and fear seeped out of her skin and got absorbed into mine, entering my bloodstream and flowing through my body, making my veins vibrate.

"You should go back inside, Avalyn," she mumbled, sort of dreamily.

I didn't move.

"We need to make sure all the windows are closed," Dad added, as hypnotized as Mom.

The massive brown cloud erased everything in its path, completely enveloping the mountains that normally blocked the wind and kept us safe from the worst of the storms. Our hills were nothing more than speed bumps in its way.

I'd only seen dust storms like this online—big, dirty woolly blankets that slowly unrolled over the flat valley of Phoenix, shrouding homes and skyscrapers and cars in a dense darkness even headlights couldn't cut through, bringing the whole city to a pause, dramatic news anchors declaring that residents needed to take cover from the coming haboob. Everyone loved using that word. At least in my house. We'd always had a good laugh about it.

But as I stared at the relentless wall closing in on us with every breath, blocking out the light and turning day to night, I didn't feel so much like laughing, especially as my chest began to ache and tighten.

This wasn't normal. This wasn't natural. Arizona dust storms didn't behave this way.

Like finding shapes in the white clouds high in the sky, I could find shapes in this brown cloud low to the earth. The shapes puffed and swirled and formed into letters in my head. I spelled so much that my brain had started finding letters in everything—the noodles on my plate, the rocks on the desert floor, the smears on the car window. And even in this terrifying cloud.

P-E-R-I-L-O-U-S.

O-M-I-N-O-U-S.

P-O-R-T-E-N-T-O-U-S.

Something was coming.

And it wasn't just dust.

# DUSTI BOWLING

is the bestselling author of *Insignificant Events in the Life of a Cactus*, *24 Hours in Nowhere*, *Momentous Events in the Life of a Cactus*, *The Canyon's Edge*, and *Across the Desert*. Dusti holds degrees in psychology and education and lives in Arizona with her husband, three daughters, a dozen tarantulas, a gopher snake named Burrito, a king snake named Death Noodle, and a cockatiel named Gandalf the Grey. She invites you to visit her online at dustibowling.com.

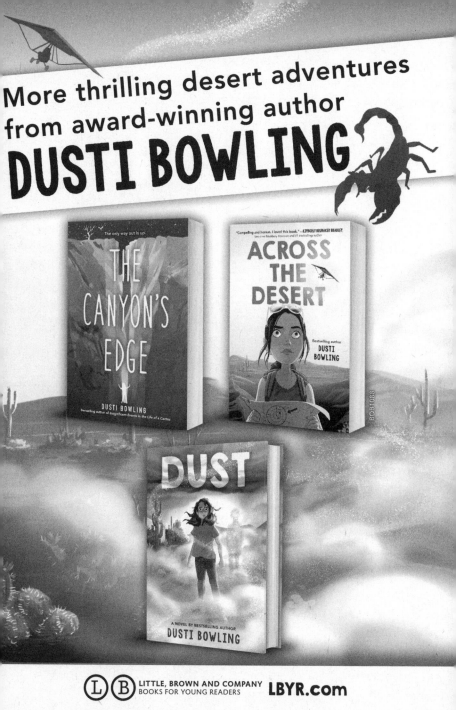